AFOOT IN A FIELD OF MEN

PAT ELLIS TAYLOR

THE ATLANTIC MONTHLY PRESS
NEW YORK

Published simultaneously in Canada
Printed in the United States of America
FIRST EDITION

Library of Congress Cataloging-in-Publication Data
Taylor, Pat Ellis
Afoot in a field of men / Pat Ellis Taylor.
(AMP fiction series)
Contents: Entering the house of the 'Lord—Who's that knocking?
Is it you?—Afoot in a field of men—Bird prayer and no amen—Answering the
inquisitor—Acquiring point of view—Descent into brotherland—Kingdom
come—Leaping Leo—Sermon on the rat—News from El Corazon : In the
composing room.
ISBN 0-87113-203-6
I. Title.
PS3570.A948A69   1988
813'.54—dc19   87-27707

Design by Laura Hough

The Atlantic Monthly Press
19 Union Square West
New York, NY 10003

FIRST PRINTING

To Morgan, Morris, and Brook

▲▲▲▲▲▲

CONTENTS

AFOOT IN A FIELD OF MEN

THE
GOD-CHASER

I don't know if a person is born to be a god-chaser or not. But there were plenty of god-chasers in my particular family, which makes me think it might be in the blood. There was my Grandmother M, after all. She was a holy roller. In Arkansas on Petit Jean Mountain holy rollers don't always handle snakes, but they do indeed roll on the plank floors of the churches. And I went to church sometimes with my grandmother, and even once saw my always jolly Uncle RC screaming and crying his way up the aisle to *repent and be saved!* flopping down across the altar rail.

In Arkansas, at least with some, this fundamental way of seeing god has also been mixed up with ess-ee-ex. They spell it out—they don't say it, they do it. So my Grandmother M rolled in the aisles, and my Grandfather M brought women to the house and told them they could stay. Then he hauled them out in the middle of the night after Grandmaw was asleep and made love to them. She locked him out. He came back, continued to woo women, etcetera, etcetera. All of the children were girls except for my Uncle RC, who was only two years older than I was. And every one of them got pregnant or married or both at an early age. Norma-Lou was the youngest. She married a holy roller preacher at the age of fourteen and is still married to him today. Wilma, the next, married at fifteen, Linda at sixteen, and my own mother at seventeen, to a man she divorced a short time later, several years before she met my dad.

The very summer my Uncle RC ran down the aisle with tears streaming down his face was the summer I was twelve and he was fourteen and we clasped each other in a mad embrace and kissed! We were supposed to be sleeping on a pallet on the living room floor, but we weren't sleeping, we were pressing our bodies together, and then pressing one hand into another one, and then pressing our mouths together into a first kiss that I remember him for to this day.

It was in my Grandmother M's living room that I read all of Uncle RC's Tijuana-Bibles, which I tucked into Grandmother M's various copies of *True Romance* and *Modern Love*. That was what Grandmother M read when she wasn't reading the Bible.

Now I myself am a marijuana smoker, and sometimes I think smoking weed might have something to do with being a god-chaser, too. Grandmother M never smoked marijuana to my knowledge, but she did dip snuff. She carried a tomato juice can with the top cut off around with her everywhere so that she could spit when she needed to. So for a holy roller, she did have her little passions.

My Grandmother T was a different story, and I really don't know that she was much of a god-chaser, but she did send out various messages. She sent out prayers with the Methodists, and scribbled notes about Art Linkletter and Jackie Kennedy on the backs of women's home magazines, as well as recipes, patterns, cures and other more cryptic phrases she would write in the margins as if alternative voices to the printed text were always coming to her, whether from a neighbor or a radio program or some more intangible air wave.

She died in a house just a few blocks away from where I am typing. I slept in the bed she had died in while she herself was lying in the coffin at the funeral home, not yet buried. And I'll say this: there was no ghost flitting around that bed. There were no angels there. Her shoes and her purse were sitting out neatly by the side of the bed when I climbed into it, as if she had decided to walk to town with another pair—as clean a getaway as you would ever hope for.

I have lain down on her grave, but only once. She didn't say anything to me one way or another. I did pick some little weedy flowers that were growing around the tombstone, and when I got home I stuck them through the eye sockets of a sheep's skull that still hangs outside my door.

My own parents wanted to be moderates. They both came from country backgrounds where church rules, and after they married and travelled to other parts of the world, they saw how there were different ways of religious thinking, and decided not to raise us in any one in particular. My father didn't go to church at all, but my mother thought we should at least go to Sunday school to hear about Jesus. She would simply choose the church nearest our house—Baptist, Methodist, Presbyterian, and the nondenominational chapels on the military bases where my father would be stationed. Then at home she made sure I got my full dose of barbarian myths to counterbalance all those god-stories I got at church, reading to me and later urging me to read the Black Forest fairy tales, the legends and ballads of German witches, fairies, giants and goddesses. But instead of making me moderate, this broad-based exposure to god-stories simply made me more curious.

One day shortly after my fifteenth birthday, I found

myself sitting in the corridor of a grand European hotel that had been confiscated by American military personnel for their own de- and em-barcations and never given back. As I recall the carpet was a plush red and the hall was quiet as a monastery row. There was a quality of twilight that lay itself in loose, misty skeins, filling all the space from the wide carpeted floor to the high sculptured ceiling above my head. I sat in a high-backed chair with carved wooden lions for my hands to cup. I was full of inarticulate emotion, in part because of my father's transfer from one side of the ocean to the other and in part because as a farewell gift to my boyfriend, in the hotel room a few hours earlier I had let him pull my panties down to my ankles and peer some minutes between my legs. So I decided that I would sit in that corridor until I saw god. I sat twenty minutes, more or less—it seemed a long time—a little nervous that my parents would come in from wherever they were and interrupt the vigil, but also striving to be filled with the stillness that was part of the twilight beginning to shape the corridor around itself. The time passed and I sat and watched and waited. Nobody came, not even my parents, and the hallway got darker, the shadows longer, the quiet quieter, until I got up and yawned a little and wondered what we were going to do for supper. God had chosen not to appear. But I think the god-chaser in my brain must have clicked on just then, because the lesson I finally learned from that instance was that after all, honey, god does not come to those who simply wait around.

AT
THE
ALTAR

When I was eighteen I flew down from Ohio to El Paso. I took the fast train out of a small and quiet university town, heading for the border like a desperado because I was so *tired* of everything.

I left my father buried in a giant snow drift—working in the basement of a granite computer building where all the wires connecting all the U.S. military bases in the world came together, sending out bullets and toilet paper, bananas, and knapsacks, powdered milk, and napalm cannisters, to all parts of the globe as his computers indicated the changing seasons of climate and war.

I left my mother behind storm windows in her farm-house in the country outside of Wright-Patterson Air Force Base, upholstering her chairs and rewiring the bathroom, retiling the floor and resewing the curtains, and recycling the roast into stew and then into hash, crocheting handbags, doilies and sweaters, canning tomatoes, and experimenting with Rice Krispies candy.

I left my friend, the theater major Sally, who wanted to be my lover. I left several thousand freshmen at Ohio University to take the empty seat in biology or economics that I was leaving behind. I left my college roommates overjoyed that they wouldn't have to put up with my slovenliness an-other semester.

I went down on the train to get some help from my uncle. He had said yes when my father called to ask if I could come to El Paso to live with him and the aunt for a little while, even though my father told him I was sick with an unknown sickness, something having to do with my head that was sending me flying out of school and home and Ohio, and into some kind of hope-I-never-see-you-I-hope-I-never-learn-how-to-circle-the-globe brand of blues.

My father was a military man, but his brother as a young man had been known as an outlaw. They grew up on an East Texas farm, but my father was quiet and a musician, while my uncle was wild and in and out of jail. But when my uncle got older he wound up in El Paso married to a large sturdy platinum blond beauty who, everyone in the family agreed, *straightened him out*. Everyone agreed if it hadn't been for the aunt the uncle would have been in prison long ago. She had been born and raised in El Paso, a town used to containing outlaws—John Wesley Hardin shot down on Main Street, Pancho Villa's head buried on the mountain. They got married and he began working for Tony Lama Boot Company, booting the feet of various Hollywood cowboys and rodeo-circuit personnel at a couple of hundred dollars a foot, and so became somewhat well-to-do: a Las Vegas regu-lar, a country-club gambler, and a generous man to his wife, buying her turquoise and a comfortable suburban house. Still my aunt continued to work as a secretary—as she had done from the time of their marriage through three children. But she had a Mexican maid.

The train from the north swooped down into Texas through Dallas and Fort Worth, and approached El Paso from the east. I was asleep when it began its descent from Van Horn at the lip of the Davis Mountains into the Rio Grande Valley. I woke up to bright morning light, and the train rolling slowly through blocks of adobe huts and mud-dried streets, brown children running in the alleys, bright clothes flapping off lines red and blue and brown.

My uncle was waiting for me on the platform, in ostrich-skin boots and a diamond-pinky-ringed hand resting on his hips—a big man with a gold tooth when he smiled and a white Stetson pushed onto the back of his head.

He met me on the train tracks and hugged me. The February sun rested on me like a robe and for the first time after months of Ohio snow I felt warm. The city of El Paso lay at the bottom of a huge beautiful red and brown clay bowl, with the Rio Grande running like a blue ceramic stripe through the middle and blending into sky at the rim.

It was a bright morning, and my uncle whisked me into his station wagon and out of the city north toward Mount Franklin.

My uncle and aunt lived right off an avenue called La Mesa, which rode along a ridge paralleling a mountain range that began to rear up just north of the Rio Grande like the shoulders of a horse with its nose buried in river water. As the road climbed higher we left the city behind. Red thunderbird cliffs startled up from the east shoulders as we drove, and on the west side rolling drop-offs—bare hills of sand and rock and cactus and crags—slid for miles down to the Rio Grande, the river at the bottom of the valley bowl that cuts a city in half. Downtown Juarez fanned out south to adobe huts scattering up into Mexican mountains on the opposite side.

My uncle drove me to the top of the Mesa rim where

he and my aunt lived. From their house I could get a good view of this panorama. They lived in a good brick home in a new suburb built on one of the highest northern ridges and named after a conqueror: Coronado Hills.

And uncle knew what was wrong with me, he could see that I just needed a little bit more room.

In the first few days of my stay he was resting up from selling boots on the road, so he took me to his resting places. He took me to the domino parlors, the dog races, the Juarez strip shows, the Alcazar Bar, where people poured wine on their heads and drank it from the streams down their noses; he took me to the bullfights and the Hofbrau Bar, where the newspaper reporters made their connections; he took me to the Juarez markets, got his boots polished for a dime, gave a nickel to the watchee-car-o to keep his car windows from being busted out, took me into halls where there were mostly men, and women dancing naked! Even the old women looked good to me on the boards, juggling their asses, dusting the air with feathers and fringe, even the little fat bulges under the fishnet and rolly thighs looked good. The women sweating and grinding dark skins in the smoky room, beautiful Mexican women with red mouths and swinging blue-black hair, such beautiful Mexican Juarez strippers. My uncle sat and smoked cigars and ordered us rounds of Dos Equis— "Amigo," he called from time to time, "*dos más por favor!*"

Uncle had some ideas of what I wanted and needed, but my aunt had some other ideas, and she knew from experience how to handle my kind of bloodline. Aunt was very sure what I really needed was a full-time job.

She was a Valhalla-mama—round, white-and-pink skin like a doll. She would put on her turquoise Southwest-style squaw dress and billow in and out of her house like a white cloud rolling around the sky just before sunset, the first pink flush of it in her skin. She was a beautiful and jolly woman, so even when you knew she was rolling right over you, billowing you right up under her hems, you couldn't get angry.

My aunt worked as an executive secretary for the El Paso Natural Gas Company, which was located in the tallest building in the middle of downtown El Paso, and she worked on the highest floor. She was able to get me a job at the gas company in practically no time, on an eight-to-five schedule, off my uncle's nighttime resting schedule.

She took me out herself the week before I went to work and showed me Playtex girdles. She told me they were the right kind of thing to buy, to get myself equipped for work with just the right kind of look. The Playtex girdle she and the saleswoman chose for me wasn't the mature woman's girdle that came down the thigh to just above the knee. This was an abbreviated version that ended just below the crotch. The girdle looked like it was made out of an ivory-colored dish drainer mat. It had little pinpoint holes all over so that your pores could gather at these openings and suck in some air.

At first I was a mailrunner. I delivered mail to the El Paso Natural Gas Company buildings scattered all over El Paso's downtown. I went out every hour with a satchel delivering mail eight times a day. I wore my girdle all the time I worked, wearing the inside of my legs red and raw when the days started heating up.

But I liked that job. My body liked the walking, my eye liked the street scenes, the cowboy boots and Mexican-brown skin mix and all the Plaza/waiting-for-the-bus jive that I got to walk through every day, all the time. My mind wheeled on its own private tours across a sky bluer than I had ever seen. Mount Franklin generated a certain clarity of light around it, like a halo that couldn't be obscured by the refinery smoke on the west side. Sometimes when I was walking the streets with my mailbag I started singing. I sang old songs from the Arkansas mountains my mother used to sing, under my breath while people passed by, and louder when I was by myself, singing to the marvelous clear sky because it felt so good to be walking around in El Paso.

But I was too good at the job. I was too cheerful, or

maybe someone noticed how well encased and rubbery indeed my buttocks were. At any rate, in just a month I was promoted and put into a little cubicle several floors above the mailroom where I was supposed to sit at a desk all day long and answer the telephone and from time to time type a letter. There was more money to it. This was called a promotion, but it was a very boring job.

I dreamed of other jobs. Before my aunt got me work at the gas company, I thought maybe I could play the piano at one of the bars my uncle took me to. I bought a book of Cole Porter tunes and began to practice on my aunt's piano. But she had gotten the job for me at the gas company so fast, and learning enough tunes to fill up an evening takes time and, like my aunt said, I needed to support myself.

After I started working upstairs at the gas company, I began to dream about the possibility of becoming a prostitute. Then I would be able to lie around my own apartment sleeping late in the mornings, writing in my diary and taking walks, then at night turning tricks. I didn't know a lot about screwing but I figured I could learn.

My aunt was methodical. She thought it would be good for me to have a job, and she was also sure it would be good if I had a man to hang out with. She knew a man—a friend of her brother's—and invited him over to the house for tacos her Mexican maid fixed for us. This man was a newspaper reporter in the process of getting a divorce. He was several years older but he had a certain glint to his eye and a fascinating way of holding a cigarette. He knew how to use words to make people listen to him, so when he talked I watched him and listened and looked hard into his one glinting eye and his one squinting eye, his newspaperman look à la Humphrey Bogart.

After my first couple of paychecks, an apartment came up for rent in this man's apartment house. He lived in Sunset Heights where three- and four-storied houses sat in clusters along twisting streets on a cliff between Mount Franklin and the Rio Grande, just a few blocks above downtown. He lived in an attic apartment painted red and black. Its ceiling slanted with the roof beams. Tall windows looked out on the singular mountain crag of Cristo Rey west of town, with its black cross dancing on top like an exclamation point in the middle of every sunset the windows framed. Pigeons camped in the eaves just above the outside shutters.

I moved into an apartment on the second floor. The sink was in the living room, my bed filled up a wooden porch with windows naturally shaded by vines.

When I came upstairs to visit the man, he put a red bulb in his reading lamp. When I began to sleep with him regularly, I sometimes waited for him at night in his bed in this red and black room while he was putting together the morning edition of the sports pages. I lit candles and watched the shadows on the red and black walls. There were also white footprints walking up one wall, over the ceiling and down the other wall into the floor. I listened to classical music and draped myself nude across his bed. Sometimes I brought a bottle of German white wine with me and set out two glasses, so that I could pour him something when he walked through the door.

I thought, when I waited for him in his black and red room, that I was making a certain kind of art, I was learning a certain kind of magic, but he was the one who had painted the room and who made the footprints and wrote the stories.

After I had known this man for a couple of months, he got a job as a sports editor on a paper in Hobbs, New Mexico. When he moved away he let me have his apartment for my own. He was lonely in Hobbs. He wrote me letters and every weekend he came back to the red-and-black apartment that had been left as he had left it—essentially the same except for my permanent occupation. His divorce hadn't even gone through, but he wanted me to marry him. He was simply too lonely living by himself in Hobbs. He said if I married him I wouldn't have to work as a secretary anymore. I could stay at home and go back to school if I wanted to. I had indeed been thinking about going to school again, because in just a few short months I had become tired of being a secretary.

Across the hall from the newspaperman's apartment lived two men who were lovers. One of the men had been born in Juarez. He was a hairdresser and an artist by the name of Gilberto. Kenny was a blond. He was a sweet and kind boy, but he really didn't seem to do much of anything except talk about life very well. Gilberto had painted a reclining nude woman eating square blue grapes along his slanted ceiling. The two men and I drank wine together sometimes and had chats lounging on pillows while the lounging nude woman stretched out over us.

Gil and Kenny took me several times across the border. They took me to the Cafe Ronny, where a tall negro with a pink afro and long green fingernails played the piano. I paid for my own margueritas and they paid for theirs. While we sat and drank and I made little shredded paper art with the cocktail napkins, they told me how foolish it would be to marry Bobby-Bee, the newspaperman, and what a sad life I would live.

"Oh I'm not going to marry him," I said. But the days were going by for me locked up in a procession of boxes—my grey office cubicle copied eight hours a day, five days a week. I went to the library and checked out anything: *The History of Western Art, Gargantua and Pantruel, Eyeless in Gaza,* you wrote it, I'll read it, and thank you for the excursion trip out of my own head, and the ticking clock on the wall, and the metal flung into the air from the opening and closing drawers of filing cabinets. I piled books on both corners of my desk. I frequented the newsstands at lunchtime and read the newspaper every morning. I bought magazines that told me what was going on in ballet in New York. I bought a Spanish phrasebook and a German dictionary. But the days sunk further into themselves and I got tired of books. At night I walked the streets in Sunset Heights and I walked in the alleys. I walked over to the highway called Doniphan Drive that led north out of town following the mountains to Las

Cruces and then up to the higher mountains—to Colorado! To Pike's Peak!

Then I blacked out. When I came to, I found myself in the back seat of a car belonging to one of Bobby-Bee's friends, the city editor of the *El Paso Times,* who was driving Bobby-Bee and me to a justice of the peace in New Mexico to get married, where you don't have to wait for three days. Bobby-Bee was sitting with me, holding my hand. He was already slightly balding and I didn't like the conservative cut of his pants. And just at that minute I believe I was in touch with every one of my historical sisters who have woken up on some heathen altar on top of a mountain with a heart beating like the rabbit sacrifice it is rapidly becoming. I thought about jumping out the back door and running like a fool, a fiend, a whole pack of dogs in one poor girl's body off across the desert. But instead I said I Do in front of a JP in the town of Socorro. The JP's wife witnessed for me.

I stayed in a Hobbs motel that evening with Bobby-Bee. He called his father in El Paso to say that he was married again. The father asked, "Is it a white girl?"

I called my mother and father, and my mother asked, "*Who* did you marry?"

I said, "Remember that man Bobby-Bee I wrote you about?" My father didn't say anything.

Oh Bobby-Bee, Bobby-Bee, he sure put a spell on me. . . .

My aunt gave us a wedding reception a week after the marriage. Her face was radiant. Her cheeks were hot pink like she had just clapped the lid on a chili pot or like the sun had come down the mountain and she had managed to catch it in the wide skirts of the turquoise squaw dress she was so fond of wearing.

The first week after I married Bobby-Bee, I opened one of his desk drawers. It was full of letters from collection agencies and past due notices and unopened bills. Lots of them were bar bills, as Bobbie-Bee did indeed have his favorite private clubs. Yes, he told me, it would be good if I went to work for a little while, because until the bills were cleared up, there really wouldn't be enough money for me to go to school or for us to go anywhere. And in fact I was already pregnant, and there wasn't any money for that, either. And newspapermen, even when they were sports editors instead of reporters, didn't make much money—didn't even make enough to cover the alcohol that fueled the word machine.

I got a job in an attorney's office. I worked as a junior secretary until the baby came.

I worked as a filing clerk in the city personnel office. Then as a secretary at the El Paso parks and recreation department. Then three months as a secretary with the El Paso Sun Kings baseball team. Two years as a secretary with Score, Hunk, Martial and Fool law offices on the top floor of the El Paso National Bank Building.

By that time I was wearing white dickey sheath dresses and three-inch heels. I never lifted anything except fingers over the typewriter keys. The heaviest labor I did on the job was lift the coffeepot.

I took night courses, read books, typed papers on my lunch breaks, pretended not to be a secretary, pretended to be somewhere else, someone else, someone reclining on a couch watching candlelight on a red and black wall, in the meantime having babies and giving them away to a Mexican maid to look over them because I wasn't a mother either. I didn't know what I was. And so I remained, suspended, for eight years. I walked like a wraith through a series of high-vaulted pyramid office buildings, through a labyrinth of carpeted hallways high up in the El Paso air, wandering in high heels through a land where the noonday heart had been removed from the calendar of my days.

▲▲▲▲▲▲

A
CLOUDED
VISIT
WITH
ROLLING
THUNDER

One time, when I was living in East Texas trying to figure out how to make a living doing nothing, I decided I would be a promoter. Of course I wouldn't be a promoter of rotten stuff, nothing porno or bad for the environment, only healthy good-for-you kinds of promotion, educational let's-learn-together kinds of things. Everybody would learn and expand their consciousness while I did the same but took a little money off the top for my extra trouble of bringing in the guru/rolfing instructor/ecstatic religious counselor, who would get the rest.

I was mostly interested in Native Americans. I wanted to hear for myself what they had to say about balanced relationships. The first people I wanted to promote were Sun and Wabun Bear from Washington state, because they had written a book that I had enjoyed called *The Medicine Wheel*, and the possibility of meeting them pleased me very much. And it pleased me even *more* when I figured I could meet them and not have to pay for it, because at the time I didn't have any money, as with many times in my particular life.

So then the possibility of me even *making* a little money began to thrill around in my head. I began writing letters and designing copy and making a poster and checking out places where the Bears could appear. I was scheming and thinking and putting pen to paper and guesstimating. I figured there could be a *huge* Texas tour. El Paso to Dallas to Houston to Austin. And of course somehow Edgewood, the town where I was living, would be along the route. After some heavy negotiating, I lined up a New Age Center in El Paso that would host the Bears. Then a ranch woman outside of Austin who was a devotee of Muktananda wanted to learn how to build a sweat lodge. I started looking around for a place in Dallas.

Nothing seemed to fall into place. So then I remembered some people I had met at the Rainbow Family gathering in West Virginia—that gathering which the Love Family and Friends put on free for thousands of people once a year. I decided to go up there and find the commune and ask if they would like to set aside a weekend for the Bears.

So I drove my truck up one day. There were a half dozen or so concrete buildings in various stages of development, and I walked up and down the mounds, and looked at the plans, and saw how all the families were putting time into their own houses and how each house was unique, revealing diverse theories of how to build a house underground—no spirit present of super-uni-development.

Some Rainbow Family people were camping there—hippie-gypsies in a wooden camper truck. Just about sunset, when the sun was dumping itself behind one of the house hills and its hobbit-style turrets, I found myself talking with a commune man named George and one of the Rainbow Family men, whose name was Majo. George was telling me that this year might be a little premature for the commune to have something like the Sun and Wabun Bear workshop but that he himself was interested in them and knew some other people would be, and maybe this next year when more of the houses were complete, something could happen like that.

Majo joined us in the middle of this conversation and was quiet while George was talking. I knew that was his name because he had been the first person who greeted me when I drove up—a thin man with tinkling little bells on ribbons and chains draped around various parts of his body. And even while George was still talking Majo distracted me. I kept looking at him because he and the sunset were more or less mingling—Majo with long and wispy gold hair and wafting beard, no shirt, purple pantaloons, red fingernails at least three inches long clicking on his crossed arms.

Then he said Sun Bear, yes Sun Bear, I've heard of him. Don't you have to pay for his workshops?

I said well yes but it's not very much.

But as soon as I heard Majo's question with the Rainbow Family point of view stamped on it, I knew I had been caught wheeling-and-dealing in matters of the heart by one of the Love Family sleuths.

George and I kept talking, but George had been caught, too. Once you've danced in the woods with the Love Family you've danced in the woods, there's no erasing that. Majo didn't say much more. He knew he didn't need to. In fact he said Oh but there are some things I would pay money for, and I have heard a lot of good things about Sun Bear and Wabun . . .

Those words didn't matter, I was back in my pick-up truck headed for Edgewood in five more minutes.

When I opened up the *Dallas Morning News* the next day there was Majo on the front page kissing Rosalynn

Carter's hand—the President's wife visiting her husband's Pentecostal sister, Ruth Carter Stapleton, who happened to live next to the underground commune. The news story under the photograph of the kiss said that somehow an unidentified man had slipped through the line of security guards, kissed her hand and made a wish for world peace.

I didn't write the Bears to tell them I had been stopped in my tracks, but I stopped working on the promotion. Everything collapsed and Sun Bear and Wabun were disappointed, and finally I moved into the city and started working temporary jobs and selling used books, and stopped trying to be a promoter. At least in that sense of the word.

▲

But this history of me as a promoter is why Rolling Thunder's people chose to get in touch with me when Rolling Thunder decided to come to Texas last winter. They wanted me to promote his tour. After the Bear thing people saw me a little bit as a promoter anyway. Even if I had failed, they didn't care, because there weren't too many hippie promoters around for these kinds of New Age/Native American workshops and weekend seminars and such, which people were beginning to want to spend their money on.

I had wanted to meet Rolling Thunder ever since I read Doug Boyd's biography of him a couple of years ago. He seemed very brave to be singlehandedly taking on the bulldozers chain-cutting the forests, and then his reputation as a powerful healer intrigued me. But I didn't want another Majo to come down on me again. So I wrote to Rolling Thunder's people, and told them that workshop fees kept spiritual information away from poor people, who needed guidance at least as much as the upper-middle-class Anglos who made up most of the audience for the national-circuit-spiritual-advisor-rounds, and that maybe the people with money could pay Rolling Thunder's way here if the workshops could be held free with requests for donations.

Someone wrote a good letter back. It was thoughtful, explaining the need of Rolling Thunder's people to support themselves. The letter let it be known that we weren't quite in agreement but still could be friends. So that was that. I was sorry I wasn't going to get to see Rolling Thunder, but I figured someone else would help him come.

Sure enough, some time later, a promoter named Cathy Lee called, to see if I could share in the promotion of Rolling Thunder's visit to Texas. He had found a sponsor in San Antonio and was scheduled for workshops there but wanted to lecture for a night in Austin as long as he was already in the neighborhood. So we talked, and I gave her this little philosophy that I had begun to put together, pretty much like I had given it to Rolling Thunder's people. We talked back and forth and she could see my point of view but she could also see Rolling Thunder's point of view, and there were many sides to the money thing. Then she said well, if I couldn't help in the actual promotion, would I like to do an interview with Rolling Thunder? She could arrange that I be paid for the piece, which would appear in the local New Age magazine. This would help in Rolling Thunder's promotion on later dates but would actually appear after he had left.

So I rolled that one around and looked at it and wondered whether it fit into my ever-cooking-and-clarifying theories of economics and spirituality. Now it was true I stood to make some money on an interview that Rolling Thunder wouldn't be paid for, but then it was supposed to be advertising for his point of view. So we both had a little money consideration—no motives are pure. And I wanted to be somewhat of a journalist/historian/writer after all, and he wanted me to put his words on paper for him, to be broadcast to a larger audience. But there was also something else bigger than any of that—*inevitability*—the call to meet Rolling Thunder, the knock on my door not once but twice. No one was asking for any money for time spent with the well-known doctor—offering *me* payment instead, provided I wrote. So I wrestled with these considerations for maybe two or three seconds before I told Cathy that Yes yes yes I would be very happy to do an interview.

Now I do like to think of myself as a journalist at

times, although every time I get around journalists I am reminded again that I am not one. They write in three hours what it takes me three years to think through. And I had never gone to a press conference before, not ever having reached that particular stage of promotion. But I figured coffee and donuts would be there, since it was in the morning, which seemed pleasant to me, and I could find a corner somewhere and simply hang out and listen to Rolling Thunder answer questions. I carried a boxful of pecans that had been sent down from my grandfather's home in East Texas, picked by neighbors to give to the visiting medicine man. On top of the box I wrote To Rolling Thunder and his family from me and mine, WELCOME HOME—the greeting used at Rainbow Family gatherings to welcome newcomers to the woods. And at eight o'clock in the morning walking along Nueces Street with a large box of pecans, with the grackles whistling and the sky clear and my hawk-feathered hat on, going to meet Rolling Thunder, I felt splendid.

But when I got to the Ni Wo Di Hi Art Gallery, no press was there for the conference except a young woman cub from the *Daily Texan* and a contingent of photographers and technicians laying out mike cords and trying out angles. I handed the box to somebody, but there weren't enough people for me to hide myself in, so I ducked into the bathroom. When I came out and there still wasn't anybody else, I decided to duck out the back door. I really wasn't prepared to ask Rolling Thunder anything. Cathy Lee caught me in the hallway. She put a tape recorder firmly in my hand, and she said that since no one else was coming I should ask Rolling Thunder some questions.

The *Daily Texan* woman and I were nervous and silent, but he sat down, lit up his pipe and began to talk, giving us over forty minutes straight on the tape recorder with very little prompting. He was a wonderful, dignified-looking man with feathers sticking out of his cap and outdoor skin and the young men of his tribe bustling around him.

But in that gallery everything was highly waxed and

framed, very inside and walled, a strange place, it seemed to me, to try talking with an Indian spiritual man. I thought well, my interview with him sure wouldn't be like that. I would ask Cathy Lee if we could have a walk by Town Lake instead while we were talking. I really began to imagine us having a very good talk together. I figured I could show him Barton Springs, the heart of Austin, and maybe even walk him to the low-water bridge to see Balcones Fault, super-spiritual crack in the earth. Then he could talk about the power of the earth and give Austin people some good words about his impressions coming to the heart of their city, healing power for the spring water. In my mind's eye I could see the young men of his tribe with whom he was traveling walking and talking with some members of my own family, a little band of us meeting together underneath the Treaty Oak on Fifth Street where warring tribes have met to work out peace terms together for hundreds of years, all of us starting out from there.

That is what Cathy Lee arranged. She said Rolling Thunder liked the idea of the walk and that maybe she herself would walk along because it was such a fine idea.

On the day of the interview I drove over to the oak tree with my husband and Brad, a young man who was living with us, and Minki the dog. Under the tree when we drove up were four of our friends with Ryan the baby. There was also a car full of men with hats and feathers pulled up to the curb, but the men were making no signs of getting out, and a young long-haired man I recognized as one of Rolling Thunder's group was talking to my friends. When he saw my car, he walked over and stuck his head in the window.

It's too noisy for Rolling Thunder here, he said. We're going back out to the Manor house where we're staying. And anyway, what is the purpose of all of these people being here with you?

They're my friends, they wanted to meet Rolling Thunder.

He said, Rolling Thunder wasn't expecting any of this,

it is entirely against protocol. You asked for the interview, you didn't say anything about bringing anyone.

I said, well, I hadn't asked for the interview, I thought *they* had wanted the interview. And I hadn't heard the word *protocol* since a childhood home built on the science-of-war and patriarchy cast me out to look for freer places. But that seemed beside the point.

I said I saw that Rolling Thunder had his tribe along with him, probably because it made him feel good to have them around, so I wanted to have some of my tribe with me.

That didn't make the young man very happy. He walked back to the Rolling Thunder car to consult. My husband jumped out of our car with the dog and said he would meet me back home later. My friends and baby Ryan were looking awkward under the Treaty Oak. I got out of the car and the young man met me in the middle of the street.

Rolling Thunder says you can bring your husband and the other one in your car, but that's all. But he's not feeling good about this whole thing.

Well I'm sorry, I didn't mean to do anything wrong.

But the young man didn't let it go so lightly. The thing is, he said, that is the problem we have with white people, always making assumptions. You should have arranged having all these people with you beforehand. You should have asked if it was all right for them to come.

I apologized again. Look, I said, I'm just a fool, I'm just ignorant. I didn't think of the right way to do things.

Well, you need to learn to call before bringing people with you. That's the correct way.

That pressed me one time too many. I didn't say anything about the six other people in Rolling Thunder's car besides Rolling Thunder. Instead I said look, let's not say it's the correct way. Let's just say it's one way of doing things, because if you were to be invited to my place (I waved at the noisy block where I had invited Rolling Thunder to meet) and brought five friends, I would say you were all of you welcome.

There we were, squared off at each other no more than ten paces away from the old Treaty Oak.

He finally said, let's not have any more trouble than we already have. Like I said, you and the people in your car can come out to the Manor house for the interview.

Okay, I told him. I don't know where that is so we'll follow you.

I got back in the car, waved to my husband and friends who were still standing at a distance trying not to be so noticeable. Rolling Thunder's car took off, and Brad took off after it. Soon we were on the freeway heading north, Rolling Thunder's car being driven like coyote himself was at the wheel, weaving in and out of the traffic so fast that Brad had to keep his foot all the way down on the accelerator and jump across lanes just to keep them in sight. And there were expired plates, an expired inspection sticker and no insurance on our car, typical protocol for my particular tribe. I figured if the police stopped us or if we crashed through the railing, that would be part of the Rolling Thunder story, too, just like the clouds rolling in from the east and the wind rising on what had seemed in the morning a warm and sunny day.

But a sign finally appeared on the road—MANOR: 3 MILES—and we were out in the country, past horse stables to a small farmhouse where Rolling Thunder and his people were already getting out of their car. It was certainly quieter and more peaceful than downtown Austin by the Treaty Oak. Even on the hike and bike trail, there would have been lots of traffic noise. I was suddenly ashamed that I had even imagined that Barton Springs would have been a good place to have talked with Rolling Thunder. While I headed for the front door with Brad, I was thinking that after all, we were getting a little time in the country away from the city. At least we were getting that, even if Rolling Thunder wouldn't talk to us. Before I could get to the house, the same young man who talked to me before stopped me again.

One more thing I need to ask you, he said, are you on your moon?

Cathy Lee had already talked to me about this. She had made sure not to schedule the interview during my menstrual cycle, on instructions from Rolling Thunder, who had told her that menstruating women had strange and static vibes that weren't good for men to be around.

I told the young man that it was all right, I had already been asked that question.

So you *did* get that part of the protocol, the young man said.

Yes, I said, feeling my face stung-red in spite of myself, I did get that.

He let me go on into the house. Rolling Thunder was standing in the living room. He looked a little tired, but he smiled at us when we came in.

I'm sorry, I said, that I arranged everything wrong for you. I guess I really didn't know what I was doing. And the country is better, it's a lot quieter out here, for sure.

Oh that's all right, he said, I think it'll be a good day anyway.

The rest of the people had disappeared. The four of us sat down. Two strange pairs: Rolling Thunder wearing his feathered hat and arranging his medicine pouch beside him, me taking off my own hawk-feathered hat as a gesture of respect for the house and laying my own pouch full of pens, pads and a tape recorder on the floor; his young man with long black hair seated near the door, my young friend Brad with his long blond ponytail and wire-rimmed glasses sitting on the couch beside me.

I said I hear you've been traveling around a lot.

He nodded. Two months of travel, then one month at home, it's been like that.

Where have you been traveling? I asked.

He said now wait a minute, you interrupted me. I wasn't finished with what I was about to say. You see, I talk slow, the people in New York—my gosh, I can't keep up with them. So you need to slow down a little bit, get into a natural rhythm. People these days are wound up tight and don't know how to slow down.

Then he started talking about chemicals in the air and the food we eat, making us half-crazy, and how white people ate all the wrong things. And you can't survive on bean sprouts and peanut butter, he said, particularly if you live north like we do. You have to eat meat if you're going to do any work. And brown bread has more chemicals in it than white bread.

Well, the dietary talk was pretty interesting, but he was telling me exactly the same things he had said at the press conference when I saw him the first time, using the same sentences and the same words almost verbatim. But since he had corrected me about interruption at the beginning of the talk, I just sat there, nodding my head, not saying anything, while he continued. I was even afraid to get my tape recorder out of my pack! I was afraid to get my notebook and pencil out! I simply sat on the edge of the couch, nodding, trying to look like I was hearing all this for the first time, while he continued for about ten minutes. Finally, apparently aware that as an interviewer I didn't seem to be doing anything, he said well, you better get your tape recorder out. Then get your notebook out and write down what I've just told you.

I felt relieved I had been given permission to set up, and so I did. He continued talking. White people are going to have to change their ways, he said, and the first thing they're going to have to change is how they treat each other. Like old people, he said. When I was in New York, I saw old ladies carrying bags with all their belongings out on the streets. And so many in unemployment lines, and so many in nursing homes and prisons. Something's out of balance, and the balance is going to have to be restored. White people could have learned a lot from Indians when they first came here about learning to live in balance, because we didn't have any of those problems ourselves.

This was a good message, a strong message, so I tried to look like they were all new words to me, even though we had sat across from each other no more than two days before while he had told it to me and the *Daily Texan* reporter in the same words. I didn't try to interrupt him in any way. I didn't even look at the list of questions on my lap. Two flies started buzzing around my head out of nowhere, the first flies I had seen since last year, landing on my nose and my mouth. I tried to wave them away, but they continued to buzz and Rolling Thunder continued talking.

He said he was a Cherokee and his people originally came from Atlantis. Part of them went to Egypt and part came to this western world, and they were a very wise race and had mysterious ways of building the pyramids.

Plus some slave labor, I said without thinking, as if some disagreeable female demon left over from my last moon had just taken over my tongue to dip a piece of loudmouth Anglo pseudo-history like a crossways oar into this riverlike monologue we had already paddled down.

No, they did *not* use slaves, he said. He glared at me, suddenly furious, pulled up in his chair. Don't *you* try to tell *me* Indian history, he said. That's the problem with you white people, trying to say what our history is. His eyes were flashing like he would have liked to have taken me apart on the spot.

It's just that I worry a little bit about empire-building regardless of where it comes from, I said, determined to own this voice as a part of myself for better or worse, since it had already spoken out. What kind of human sacrifice it took.

Well, Rolling Thunder wasn't named that for nothing. He let me know for a good several minutes that he was displeased with my presence and my approach. He said I had no respect, and that was the trouble with white people. White people had the Inquisition, why didn't we talk about that? He asked me if I wanted to just be a writer or if I wanted to be a great writer, and if I wanted to be a great writer, then I had better stop looking at the bad and start looking at the good. Usually people who were going to interview him were given a list of questions that they could ask him and that when it came to me, someone had really goofed. He didn't like people making jokes about being ignorant either and that when people didn't have the right kind of attitude he usually just threw them out. And he continued glaring at me like he was going to do just that.

I figured the interview couldn't get any worse and that

to die from Rolling Thunder's thunder would be as good a way to go as any. Besides, I had heard this tone of voice before from my own military father, except that he used to tell me my problem was being a stubborn female rather than being white. So I said well, the only reason I brought this all up is because in this part of the country, when you talk about going back to the old Indian ways of doing things, you might be talking about Cherokee or you might be talking about Aztec, and it's probably good to sort out one kind of Indian ways from another.

There was a little silence. He looked at me. Then he looked out the window.

They went down, he finally said, apparently referring to the Aztecs, because they abused their own power. They brought themselves down. Look, when I want to feel better, I can just look out this window, look at the trees, the grass, that settles my mind.

He looked out the window some more. I did, too, following his example. The thunder stopped and the atmosphere began to settle.

Well, would you talk a little about how you came to be a medicine man?

No, he said, I don't like to talk about that.

Too personal? I asked.

He nodded. He was quiet for a little bit. He was tired of the interview and tired of me.

Maybe I will say something about it, he said finally, mustering up the powerful forces of his own good humor. I knew that I was going to be a medicine man from the beginning, he said, except that's not what we call it. We don't say medicine man. And I had to go through seven trials in order to become one—

Just then the door burst open, and a tall man stumbled in, eyes glazed over like he didn't know where he was, or like a drug-sick man looking for strong medicine. Rolling Thunder's young man, who had been sitting quietly through the interview, got up and started pushing him back outside. You don't belong here, he said. The tall man fell into him, then into the couch, leaning this way and that, while the young man got him out the front door again.

The vibes don't seem to be right today, Rolling Thunder said.

Yes, I said. I think you're right.

The flies still buzzed around my head. I can't even get these flies to stop bothering me, I told him, quite aware that the only flies were on my side of the room. I looked down at the tape recorder. The tape was tangled up in the sprocket and wads of tape were coming out of the top.

Well, Rolling Thunder, I said, is there *anything* white people have to contribute?

Well yes, he said. But then he thought a long time before he said anything else. Well, he said finally, money is all right. It depends. People say that money is the root of all evil, but it depends where it comes from and where it's going.

And that is all he said.

So Brad gave him the tobacco he had brought for a present, and I packed up my bag. The tape recorder's tape was frazzled and no good. The only part that had been recorded was the part that I had already recorded at the press conference, the message he wanted everyone to hear, the words he considered important enough to repeat and repeat: that white people are out of balance, they need to change, and that the first thing to change is how to get along with each other.

Well, I told him, once I had gotten my bag back together as much as I could, this has been a special afternoon for me because I've always wanted to meet Rolling Thunder.

He smiled broadly, then began asking me some questions, friendly and kind, about the feather in my hat and whether or not I was part of the Rainbow Family. I told him I knew them. I wasn't exactly a part, but related. I told him that I was also supposed to be a little Cherokee. Just about everybody from Texas, I said, is supposed to be a little Cherokee.

Oh yes, he grinned, I remember the braves coming off the reservations making raids down here when I was young.

We said that if the Cherokees couldn't take the land with war, they would take it by love.

Indian raids.

I kept smiling and nodding, but whatever gulf there was between us had just widened. My head was suddenly alive with all the stories I had ever heard from my own East Texas blood relatives about settling wild country and witnessing massacre and death administered by Indian raiders. Rape and kidnapping! But after he recalled that little piece of history, I looked at him briefly square in the face, and even with the Indian raid horror stories around him like an antique robe, he was a beautiful, old, wise and strong-looking man to me. He was as smiling and good-humored as my own East Texas grandfather had been, someone who had also found his peace in looking out at the land. He puffed on his pipe, and had a mild smoker's cough from smoking his pipe with so many strange people on this tour he'd been doing for months of white man's cities. *Even though he charged money I liked him.*

He asked some other questions, and said some polite leaving things, but I could only answer in monosyllables as I moved toward the front door, off balance and dizzy, not much better than the crazed man who had been shown out just a few minutes before me. There was no New Age, and I was no promoter nor any interviewer either, I was the oldest grand-daughter and Rolling Thunder was the youngest grandfather but there were still some generations to reach across, and we were male versus female, we were white versus Indian. We weren't friends, we were almost enemies, we were the heads of two parallel histories coming up on different banks of the same river—the River Versus—strange waters we didn't know yet how to cross.

▲▲▲▲▲▲

SPRING
WATER
CELEBRATION

Close to springtime, and there was a certain undercurrent of fever and bustle in everyone, like I imagined was building in the seeds and roots and all underground, preparing to come rushing down and up and out. But it was heating up too fast, no rain for weeks, over eighty degrees one day after another, too hot for young plants. I talked to the Austin goddess followers to see if I could help them plan a spring celebration at a spring, and we decided on a little pool of water called Sunken Gardens, with a gravel bed shaped like a womb, and three-fourths circled by tiers of earth, opening toward the

Barton Creek side. Barton Springs, heart flow of Austin water, where hippie women bathed topless years before other parts of Texas ever saw a public boob, was only yards away. Barton Springs was closed for the first time in any spring because of a too-high bacterial count from shopping center sewage runoff, running hot. Shit Creek, as they say, with no paddlers. The goddess followers said we could have a picnic in a cedar grove nearby. We would parade ourselves over to the spring and meet at 4:56 P.M. on March 20, clocktime for the spring beginning. There would be some dancers and musicians and we would wind around Zilker Park, where the frisbee people and the dog walkers and barbequers and shade-tree poets and all would also no doubt be. These people might then feel compelled, upon seeing us a-trooping, to join in for the walk to the springs. Then at the springs we would have a celebration.

I didn't know exactly what kind of celebration there would be at the springs, and it seemed important that nobody knew what celebration there would be, so that whatever magic happened would come from this particular water joined for this particular springtime with these people who were naturally drawn together for whatever reasons of their own. No borrowed rituals or ceremonies. No set words. The flyer sent out for the occasion said only that there would be a water celebration with one hour of spontaneous words. So I figured everyone would bring their magic stuff, whatever it was, and I started collecting mine. First a friend and I went around to the flower shops in town and got some big bunches of throwaway flowers: beautiful daisies, red gladiolas, yellow snapdragons, long-stemmed roses saved from the garbage piles. We put them in a basket, I tied on a goat bell found by a friend in the West Texas desert, and I put on a long white robe embroidered with flowers my own poet-lover Leo gave me after his last trip to the southern Rio Grande. My son Chico brought a flute, Leo put a water poem in his pocket and carried a blue and white wind sock; and so we started out.

The day was grey not sunny. When we got to the

goddess-followers' picnic, they were milling around, unsure of what to do. I started giving out the flowers. Two women dancers got up and said they were going to lead the parade. They said the parade should be silent, that no one should say a word, that we should make deliberate steps and breathe in and breathe out in a deliberate manner, concentrating on breathing in spring and breathing out winter, or something along that line. There were about twenty people in all. There was a guitar player and a fiddler, and they had been playing some music when we first got there, but they put their instruments in cases and carried them quietly when the parade began.

No one really gets much into following a silent parade unless it's a wake for a friend (an elegy for an unclean pool) so the rest of the park people ignored us as we paraded behind the two silent high-stepping dancers leading the breathing and the two musicians with their instruments encased. But the goat bell slammed against the flower basket I was carrying, and I felt a little like a goat myself tripping along. Leo's wind sock floated above the procession on the path leading through bushes and trees just beginning to leaf themselves out.

When we got to the spring another group of people was waiting there for us. Grey Eagle from Dallas, Ed Ward and Marsha with Passion the baby, Dorothy the goddess missionary, the sun mother Margaret, a woman with a feather stick, several others ranging themselves along the rock and earth shelves. I got up on a ledge and started talking. I told about Balcones Fault, the long crack in the earth Austin is built on, where Barton Springs the springs rise, where people have lived for hundreds and maybe thousands of years, believing it a special and powerful place to be—putting out fumes of Austin mellowness in the air—an appropriate place for legislators trying to work out agreements to converge upon. And then I said some things about the pollution, how sad it was that we should forget our water is a reflection of our own state of health, and that it was time to give something more to water than our sewage. The talk wasn't very coherent, and not very celebrational. But then there was a song, and the flute player started playing his flute and the fiddler got her fiddle out, and the guitar player began strumming, and people threw flowers into the spring and I threw in the rest of the basketful.

The water didn't look too good. It was the lowest I had ever seen, not even high enough to flow out of its opening into the creekbed. I had brought a bucket in case people wanted to baptize themselves, but after so much publicity about the sewage, baptism didn't carry the weight of its cleansing and purifying metaphors too well. How could there be a water ceremony though without water? While everyone was chanting and singing, looking down from their dry perches into the water, this question continued to come to my mind. So I kept peering into the water, trying to see something—how polluted it was or wasn't, and if it smelled at all, and what the stuff was mixing with the flowers floating on top of it. Next year have a water ceremony at a local swimming pool maybe . . . in somebody's hot tub . . . back home underneath the shower. Then I looked around at everybody looking beautiful and dry. No magic in a water ceremony without water; that was the strong message coming to me. So I crawled down to the stone opening where the water would have been flowing out if it had been deep enough, grabbed my bucket, took off my shoes and waded in. I walked out into the middle of the pool. The water was cool and smelled good, like water. There were flowers everywhere, and I thought well, water is polluted everywhere, water that comes out of the tap is polluted after all, and this water has just been blessed with dozens of flowers coming from dozens of good people, and if it makes me sick, it makes me sick, I don't care. Someone said Take your robe off! And so I did. There I was nude in the middle of the pool with flowers everywhere. I ducked down and ducked down again and floated around and it was cold but not too cold. I called out to the people standing around, Don't be afraid of this water! Then Marsha Ward was at the

35

spring opening, her clothes already shed. She started splashing around, too, and after her came children wading in a little bit at a time and a young man who got his ankles wet and a woman to keep the flowers floating.

The day was grey. No one really knew what to do without a printed program. We all come from different traditions when it comes to magic, and our songs and vocabularies are strange and unfamiliar to each other. I wasn't even sure the magic had come until I got out of the pool and someone gave me a shawl and we started walking to the car. Then I realized that there had been a message from the water: it was underneath my own skin now, my hands cool to everyone I touched, my body cool and calm. The message was SLOW DOWN; COOL OFF; PEOPLE EVERYWHERE THIS SPRING SHOULD CONCENTRATE ON COOLING DOWN. The sky was grey and getting greyer, and a cool breeze was coming up, and while we were driving home, the first raindrops misted across the windshield, the first rain in weeks, which would continue steady for seven days, bringing the temperature down into the sixties, spring magic for the most skeptical, of the best kind.

▲▲▲▲▲▲

TURNING
THIRTY-EIGHT

Morgani was going to be eighteen in June. He wrote me a long letter. He was in El Paso living with his dad, and I was living with Leo in East Texas, seven hundred miles away. Still, he wanted me to come so we could celebrate his birthday together. And Morgani, I knew, had thought about becoming eighteen since he was thirteen years old, wondering what kind of a man he was going to become. Now that the birthday was almost here, he could see he was working at grocery checkout and practicing his music full-time, and that is the kind of a person he had grown up to be. I knew he sometimes had a

37

hard time dealing with that, because all his close friends were doing other kinds of things. They were going to college or learning a trade. But Morgani was dyslexic and he had played the guitar since he was eight years old and he was a musician. He had decided that about himself. All of us, his dad and Leo and me and Morgani, too, knew that he had chosen for himself a very difficult way.

Well, I really didn't want to go to El Paso. Morgani had been living with his dad since the first of the year, and although this dad and I were tolerably jolly around each other after so many years and remarriage on both sides, still, we weren't close friends. In June I was supposed to be in Austin anyway, doing research for a manuscript that was supposed to be completed by the first of July. So I thought to myself, how important is it, really, that I be there for his birthday? Don't I have a tendency to make myself out as more important than I really am—a basic human tendency? After all, I have no doubt he loves me. Still and all, if I tell him I just can't come he'll be a little disappointed, but he'll have lots of friends there and his father and his grandparents on that side, etcetera etcetera. They're bound to throw him a big birthday party, bigger than anything I could give him, because they've done it many times in the past. He's bound to get lots of presents and really have a very good time.

Morgani, I said, I just can't do it. I just can't come. I gave him the list of reasons I had put together.

Mom, he said, after I finished (his voice has gotten really deep the last couple of years, so to my ear he sounds like he's doing an imitation of a deep voice because his real voice should be much higher), without you there won't be anybody.

Mothers my age have been hounded by Freud since wielding our first diaper pins. We are especially careful not to show too much concern for our sons lest we be accused of female perversion. Still, when I realized Morgani actually wanted to spend his eighteenth birthday with me, his mother, this pleased me at a very basic level and made me enormously happy.

Why don't you come to Austin then? We could meet each other there.

Well I probably could.

He was beginning to brighten up. Dad could give me the money for my birthday present. I could take off work for a couple of days.

We could do Austin together. I'm not really big on bars, but we could do that for a little. I could buy you your first legal beer.

I'm not really into bars either, Mom.

I knew he wasn't; still, doing a few bars might be a little fun when your son was turning eighteen.

But as soon as I hung up, I began to worry. Where were we going to stay in Austin? We weren't going to stay anywhere, that was part of our plan; anywhere, at least, that would cost us money. The truth is that Leo and I have been writing stories and poetry for a while. And we don't make a whole lot of money at it. In fact, that's why we moved to East Texas in the first place, so we could get cheap housing and grow some of our own food, so we could live pleasantly without having to give up writing for some kind of work that actually paid. So for Austin we had a van with a tiny camper, and we simply planned to park it at a curb. And we were not naive about this. We knew that camping on a side street for several weeks in Austin could very well be against the law. But it couldn't be a very expensive law. Probably the worst that could happen would be that a policeman would come and give us a ticket for loitering or illegal parking. That would probably be no more than twenty-five dollars, or the cost of a motel room for a night. The best probability was that we wouldn't be given a ticket at all but simply told we had to move on. This had seemed a good plan when Leo and I had talked about it for ourselves. But when I tried to imagine Leo and Morgani and me, three large bodies packed into a space the size of a closet, sleeping together, eating together, and finally bursting balloons and giving presents and having a birthday party parked at an Austin curb, the picture took on a kind of Mad Hatter quality that wouldn't go away. And

39

then, as I say, there wasn't any money. Maybe enough money for a couple of beers but not for anything else. What were we going to do for this birthday? How could I have promised to "do" Austin with him when there weren't the means available to do anything at all? So I worried all the while that Leo and I were packing the van. At least, I consoled myself, Morgani would have an airplane flight for his birthday. That could be exciting even if we happened to spend the night in jail on vagrancy charges. After all, this life is my life, I thought defensively, and I am his mother. And so I continued to stew.

When Leo and I drove into the Austin city limits, it was dark. We knew where the campus was and we headed for that. About five blocks away from the campus entrance, we found a quiet side street. In the middle of the block was a large vacant lot overgrown with trees, with a little bit of a sidewalk in the parking area, the perfect place for a camper to park. We idled right up to the curb and turned off the lights. The street was dark and peaceful, lined with trees made into silver silhouettes by one tall streetlight. A large yellow cat walked up to see who had parked. When I lowered my arm out of the window, he sniffed it, then rolled himself on his back on the little piece of sidewalk with his paws up toward me and began to purr. Leo and I took this for a sign that this must be the right place to park. And this is where we stayed for the next three weeks.

By the time we were supposed to meet Morgani's plane, the day before his birthday, we had established a regular routine. Each morning when we jumped out of the camper door we said hello to our new neighbors loading in their cars to go to work. We freshened up at Mr. Gatti's Pizza right around the corner, and we bought hot coffee at Winchell's, on The Drag. We didn't cook hot foods because we didn't want the van to smell too domestic. We bought yogurt and cheese and granola bars and juices and kept it simple that way. A pan of water, hand pumped out of our holding tank, wasn't exactly a shower, but made enough water to lather soap. We worked at the library until it closed in the evenings, then sometimes went out for a glass of wine before going back to our block. At night we bedded down. The top had a window that cranked up so we could look out through a few little branches to the Austin night sky.

When Morgani got off the plane, he was wearing a black derby hat. His hair was down to his shoulders, and looked like he had blow-dried it. He wore a yellow T-shirt that said World's Oldest Hippie, which I distinctly remembered as belonging to his younger brother, and he was grinning in a large, happy kind of way. As he walked down the ramp from the plane, he seemed very tall and big muscled. This is still new enough to be a surprise. When I saw him, I began to worry less. After all, he was my son, he wasn't someone else's, and he was used to adapting to strange routine. We picked up his luggage—a backpack and his guitar—and headed back to town.

Up to that point I hadn't told Morgani Leo and I were staying in downtown Austin in the camper. I was afraid his dad would find out and would call me and ask me questions in the you-have-got-to-be-kidding-me tone that was a primary symptom in our marriage's demise. But driving Morgani to our campsite, I mentioned it to him. You know we're going to be sleeping in this thing, Morgani, I don't know if I told you or not.

Oh, that's fine, he said as nonchalantly as if I had told him we had booked rooms at the Sheraton, the band and I have been sleeping in a van together when we go out of town to play. He peered at the space behind us. Looks like there's plenty of room.

Oh there is, I said, sounding like I thought there really was. I thought you wouldn't mind. And why had I ever thought he *would* mind? Because, I realized, I was a mother, I wasn't eighteen years old; because I was in my thirties and certain kinds of things seemed bizarre, even though I was the one doing them, while to Morgani life was life, nothing was bizarre at all.

Leo pulled up to our place and we began to show

Morgani around. We walked up to the end of the block one way and then we walked down the other. Traffic sounds came from far away, but it was eleven o'clock at night and we were the only people around. The sound of our footsteps seemed comradely, walking together. The yellow cat came out and lay down on the sidewalk when we walked by the frame house where he lived. We showed Morgani the little garden we had discovered on the back part of our lot and finally we took him up to Mr. Gatti's for a cup of coffee before we went to bed. There was a pile of bodies, all right, but it was comfortable enough. I went to sleep to the intertwined tones of two snores.

In the morning I woke up before they did. Leo was stirring, a little bit out of the sheet covering him. But he seemed determined not to open his eyes and admit to being awake. Morgani still seemed very asleep. His body was only partially covered by his sheets, and I studied the curly hair that grew all over it. It really was amazing, all that hair, although there still weren't enough whiskers on his face to grow a mustache or a beard. I wished I had a stack of presents I could have piled on top of him, things expensive and significant to a boy entering adult life—a new electric guitar or the keys to a new car or even a wristwatch. But I didn't have anything like that. Instead I got a rolled-up poster out of the glove compartment that I had bought at a head shop closeout sale. It showed a giant burrito being clumsily flown off the ground into the sky by a heroic pilot. The caption said By jove, I believe he's flying that burrito, it's a giant burrito taking off from the ground! I was ashamed I didn't have anything else. But I had wrapped it up and tied it with red yarn, so it looked festive.

I began singing Happy Birthday, and Leo helped me finish the last two lines, and then Morgani woke up. I gave him the poster.

Thank you, Mom, he said. He said this with a little formality, as if receiving a certificate or an award.

I've got something else for you, too. I pulled out two

joints of Colombian marijuana. For your birthday, I said. So we crammed ourselves knee to knee along the sleeping cot in our underwear feeling happy, smoked, and handed around a can of peaches. Then we pulled on T-shirts and washed ourselves and shared a comb. When we jumped out of the van's back door, I was sure we looked as presentable as the governor's family.

Leo was going to spend the day at the library. He had to get his poems ready for a poetry reading that evening. Now don't think you have to go to my poetry reading, Morgani, he said. After all, it's your birthday, you should do what you want. Morgani and Leo had had their ups and downs in the past, uneasiness always certain to happen with a new marriage and a half-grown son. But Morgani, today, was feeling eighteen. He was ready for poetry. No, Leo, he said, that's all right. I'd like to hear you read. Then afterwards we can go somewhere and hear some music. Is that all right?

We agreed to meet again at the camper around five o'clock. Leo took off down the block. Suddenly some of my original misgivings came back. Here we were, and what would we do now? When was the last time I had spent a whole day alone talking with Morgani? Maybe, really, never before in our lives.

Well, Morg, would you like to go to Oat Wille's?

Aw, not really, he said. I don't have any money to spend.

We could look at instruments around the corner at the music store.

Naw. We were standing at the curb. There was plenty of sunshine, but it was a cool morning. The combination of heat and breeze was a good one on my shoulders and face. I tell you what, Mom, he said, let's just walk around some.

Of course. He was my son and like me, he liked to walk. He pointed a way and we took off together. First we walked to the capitol. We looked at the squirrels and the pigeons, and we kept right on walking through downtown to the river. At the river we made a discovery. There was a hiking and biking trail that could take us east and west, or north and south, for several miles without ever having to intersect with a regular road. So we decided to walk this path west and then come back east on the other side of the river. For walking along the river, I had what I thought was a dandy hat, a straw hat I had bought in a K-Mart a few weeks before. It had a brim like a Humphrey Bogart felt, and a long brown feather that stuck out of the hatband on one side. Wearing that hat and my good set of clogs, walking along with my very good-looking son, I felt pretty cocky.

So Morgani and I walked along the river path together. At first we talked about his brother and sister a little, because they were staying with his dad, too, for the summer, and I wanted to get caught up on their news. Then he began reminiscing. Remember Uncle Gary, he began, when all of them lived with us until he fell off the roof and got saved?

Well yes, I remembered Gary.

And remember after Dad left, us living with Eleanor and not even having enough money for toilet paper? Now those were some hard times.

All of my children like that particular story. When I first started graduate school, in the mornings I would advise them to take a little extra paper from the toilet dispensers at school and stick it in their pockets for home use. Food stamps didn't cover paper products, and all of our money went to house and utilities. So we walked along and talked about the eighteen years we had been together. Always before when I thought about these times, I had felt a sadness that I had put my children through them, because there had been my own growing up to do with their growing up. When I started meditation, Morgani had gotten a mantra, too. And then when I decided that Western civilization should come to terms with the Christian church and started going to Pentecostal revival meetings, Morgani went along, too. Later when I stayed home again, then Morgani stayed at home, too. And there was a bankruptcy, a divorce, graduate school, and finally a remarriage. And what an embarrassment, my own growing up! How much better if I could have taken to a closet for those years and gone through my transformations where my children couldn't see me.

But this was Morgani's birthday, and he was calling all the history back. I had thought it was mine, but it was his, too. This time it didn't seem as sad as before. This time, in fact, it seemed a little funny. And I thought, after all, children become like their parents; there are very few surprises. I am somewhat eccentric, there is no doubt of that, and so of course will my son be eccentric. And walking in the capital city of Texas along the river that was blue, passed every once in a while by an earnest, sweating jogger, I thought how much Morgani was like I was when I first turned eighteen and came to El Paso. And how very wonderful it could be, despite the drawbacks, to have had a baby before I had turned twenty. Maybe, in my growing up, I hadn't done so well at times for my children. But I did as well as I could, and for the first time I thought that was all right. I excused myself a little. Because here I was on this day, walking and talking with my son.

So we looked at the flocks of ducks swimming in the river and observed the canoers doing well downstream and struggling going up. We walked through the Japanese gardens on a meditation path, and then we walked to Barton Springs. We talked about my book and my stories and my big dreams, and he talked about his guitar and his songs and his big dreams. And even when it was evening, we continued to walk. We walked to Leo's poetry reading and afterwards we walked the university Drag and listened to music and bought Morgani's first legal beer.

Do you know what a pitcher of "draft" means? I asked him.

He shook his head. That's why I need you, Mom, to explain all these things.

Finally we walked back to the camper. Leo was walking with us then. He was happy about reading poetry, all of Austin was a lyric he was humming as we walked along. By 11:45 we were pulling off our clothes and settling into bed.

Well, Morg, I said, Happy birthday. You were born just this time eighteen years ago. It was almost June fifteenth by the time you got around to being born.

I was late, wasn't I? he said.

So I knew he wanted to hear the story again. I told him that he was little and very ugly and red. Then I told the part about how the nurse had finally brought him out naked so that I could dress him and take him home, and I didn't even know how to put the diaper on him. I worried a little about telling this story while Leo was there because it seemed sentimental, and I was afraid he would make fun of it. But Leo was quiet while Morgani listened and tried hard to comprehend himself as a small baby. Finally we were quiet. He stuck his foot into my side and wiggled it into the sheet.

Have you ever flown a burrito before? he asked.

Many times, Morg, many times.

Your mother, Leo said, was flying a team of huevos rancheros when we first got together. I was attracted to the way she could handle an egg.

It was past one o'clock. Outside the camper came a faint whizzing sound. I looked out the little window along my side of the van and saw the dark shapes of two young boys tossing a frisbee back and forth in the street. Leo and Morgani raised themselves up to see what I was looking at, and we remained silent, unknown to the boys, as they tossed the saucer back and forth, back and forth on the quiet, cat-guarded block in the middle of the night. When I lay back down, I could still hear the disc for a long time near the camper, whistling.

▲▲▲▲▲▲

AN
INDEPENDENT
MEDITATION

When Leo and I finally make the move to Austin, center-of-
the-Lone-Star, we set up business no more than six blocks
from the capitol grounds due south, selling used books out
of an old warehouse on a short-term lease and cooking on
our-home-on-the-range in the basement. Everywhere else
downtown the rent is too expensive, and the real estate devel-
opers have designs on this old warehouse district like they
have all over—master schemes for every inch of downtown.
But they are concentrating their efforts closer to the capitol
right now, so it's still a few months before the wrecking balls

come to this neighborhood. Meanwhile weeds grow in the parkways. Windows are boarded up on some of the blocks. Most of the action comes after dark when the bars open—gay bars with entrances in the alleys and catwalks into cellars, wino bars with plank floors, transvestites at night in the parking lots leaning against car hoods with their asses up, drunks crumbling when the dawn is nearing, rocking themselves to sleep in vomit pools.

At first, I get sick for a while. I don't want to leave my basement room. I don't want the basement light on, and I don't want to see anybody. My kids have gone different places. I think about the basement's pipes and the city's sewer lines, the streams and rivulets in the ground just the other side of the basement's concrete walls—natural rivers, piped rivers, rivers of water, rivers of wire, rivers of gas and electrical currents, rivers of legislators' toilet flushings. Leo brings me cups of coffee when he isn't working with the books upstairs. Pretty soon I get better, then start working, selling books again. There aren't many customers and most of the day the bookstore is quiet.

At night after the bookstore doors are closed and the tabs are run, Leo and I take walks. Sometimes we walk south right out of the warehouses, down a grassy bank to watch the Colorado River slosh around in the present dammed-up form the engineers have dreamed for it called Town Lake. We watch the sunsets, and the ducks on the water struggling through flotillas of beer cans and paper cups and eddies of phosphorescent slime.

Other nights we walk north, right up Congress Avenue to Dunkin-Donuts. We buy coffee and sugar-coated dreamboats and walk to the capitol so we can browse on the grass and watch the squirrels.

The grass is cool. The shadow of trees on the capitol-ground strollers below the branches is the sweetest of balms, licking the excess heat of the day off the skin like dark tongues. Crickets sing. One starts and then some others, all together, then all together stop. The squirrels bound across the grass full of that kind of confidence that comes only from inheriting land wealth, having ancestors unswayed by the increase in human industry. I walk around the ground barefoot. I pad alongside Leo on the Congress Avenue sidewalks, and then when we come to the capitol I shuffle through the grass and enjoy the cool of the ground.

Leo doesn't suggest going inside the capitol building for the first couple of months we are in Austin, even though we visit the grounds two or three times a week. I don't suggest it either. But sometime after Dunkin-Donuts on Congress closes its doors for good and I am trying to get over my grief that there is no other place to get a donut and a cup of coffee at night in all of downtown, I tell Leo I want to go inside the capitol building.

He says why.

I say well, I want to go into the capitol building so that I can see the Texas Declaration of Independence with Richard Ellis's name written on it.

Well, Leo says, I'll wait outside.

So he waits outside. I walk up the capitol steps onto the marble lobby floor, which is cool and smooth under my feet. Sure enough, I see a little lighted window with the Texas Declaration of Independence behind the glass on a lever so that the pages will turn without being touched as the paper slowly disintegrates with time. I try to read it, but the words are blurred and I know that Leo is waiting outside, so I think to myself Oh I can read what it says at the library, it doesn't matter that it has become illegible. I skip to the end and read the first name signed and sure enough, the name—Richard Ellis—is there, black and big like he knew exactly what he was up to.

Now when I was growing up my father, Texas Aggie military man that he was, siring military brats all over the country, kept gathering us up in his lap to tell us about Texas, the land we were from. He told us he grew up in the Free State of Van Zandt, a county of farmers, called the Free State, he said, because the people there were so ornery they wouldn't submit to the North and wouldn't join the South. And he told us about Richard Ellis the first signer of the Texas Declaration of Independence, who, he assured us, was our great-uncle. Or great-great-uncle. At any rate he was great, and he was an Ellis and that was a fact.

My father loved Texas, he knew the military life was just a phase. There would be a day that would come when he would retire and then he would come back to East Texas and maybe he would buy a farm.

Every summer when we could, when we weren't overseas or somewhere too far up north living with the Yankees, my father put all of us in the car so that we bratty kids could have a little taste of Texas, we could visit Grandmaw and Grandpaw on the farm and eat yellow-meated watermelon. Grandpaw didn't own the farm, he was a sharecropper, but I didn't know the economic nuances of that fact until I was grown. He played the fiddle and my father accompanied him on the guitar and I chewed sugar cane and listened to them play far into the evening. And to me that was what Texas was all about.

So I stand in front of the glass case and look at the name Richard Ellis for a while. I simply dwell on his name with my eyes like I am trying to read his character. I am trying to see the thoughts that were in his mind when he was signing. I look at his name a good five minutes, even though I know Leo is pacing around thinking those mixed kind of Yankee-come-to-Texas thoughts that I know have their intellectual validity but that have no root in my soul.

Now the truth is that Richard Ellis really is not my ancestor. I found this out only a short time ago. My father, in his retired Texas years, has searched out family roots and made charts. He doesn't have a farm, but he has a stone house on a cliff in the Texas hill country that a life given to the military bought for him and my mom.

The last time I went home and sat in his Kerrville living room, watching the Guadalupe River swing through his backyard, I said something about that good ol' great-uncle ancester Richard Ellis, and my father said Well, you aren't a direct descendant of Richard Ellis, but I know there is a family connection.

I was shocked but tried not to show it, and my father looked a little sad that he had to tell me such bad news. As a historian he has to stick with the facts as they become revealed. Still, I can look at Richard Ellis's signature for a full five minutes even though I know we are not connected by any direct line, even though the marble floor is beginning to make my feet cold. Too much air conditioning in the dome.

I know my friend Ricardo would never be caught dead inside this capitol building. I know that I have no friend ever made in hippie kingdom or university, in bookstore aisles and other places of random learning who would stand with me in front of this glass trying to figure out what Richard Ellis was thinking when he signed his name. They would all be out there in the grass watching the squirrels with Leo, every one of them.

Ricardo came into the bookstore not too long ago with a good Anglo-liberal friend from somewhere else. Maybe North Carolina. Some grant-writer friend. It was shortly after the Fourth of July and this friend of Ricardo's said Well, I don't celebrate it.

I said you should.

He said, Well after all, what is it really declaring?

And I said Independence!

I never could figure out what he wanted me to say.

But then I've spent too many years thinking about Richard Ellis being part of my direct line. I know if anyone put a Declaration of Independence in front of me, I would be the first to sign it.

Can't we all use a little more independence? I mean nobody celebrates the day Texas joined the Union, no big deal. Pass the petition around again today, maybe this time Ricardo and his friend will sign it, too. I'll pass them the pen, Ricardo's got Richard Ellis in his name as much as I do.

I can look at that signature for a long time. But I stop

because I get tired of being foolish and I'm glad no one else is in the foyer to see me gazing at the Texas Declaration of Independence with hot-hot romance in the eye, swept off into dream realms by the bold stroke of a dead man's signature. So I pad across the inlaid star and through the doors outside to the muggy Austin night and down the steps into the tree-cooled grounds. Leo is sitting on a cannon with his arms crossed.

Well did you see it, he asks.

I saw it. It was pretty interesting.

What does it say?

Oh, it says something about human rights and about not wanting to fight a foreign country's war, I say, trying to think of some part of the document that I had managed to make out.

And was Richard Ellis's signature there?

Yep, it was there all right.

He doesn't say anything. I don't say anything either. We walk under the arching trees down the sidewalk, down Congress Avenue, where the storefronts are being leveled for the bank buildings to grow on top of, where the little businesses, like used bookstores and all-night coffee shops that rent instead of own, are being edged out one after another. I watch where I'm walking, the sidewalk a river of concrete, glass, spit and chewing gum, the silent city underground, rivers whispering up through the soles of my feet. Oh I would sure make some changes along these sidewalks if I had my way.

▲▲▲▲▲▲

ENTERING
THE
HOUSE
OF
THE
'LORD

So here I am, living with Leo in East Texas, about sixty miles out of Dallas on the edge of a very small town. At first it is all right. We don't have to pay rent, we keep chickens, we have a garden, and we write a lot. But then the money runs out. The truck breaks down, the plumbing breaks down, the garden rake breaks, the dishes break, Leo breaks me over his knee, I break every promise I ever made to him, and no money in the house for fixing anything. Two of my kids off to El Paso to live with their dad. Later on they will tell me how they got used to having sausage every morning with their eggs. Only Morgani stays. He's already been in El Paso with his dad. He's a high school dropout, his eyes weird, unable to focus right, so it's not easy for him to get a job in a border city like El Paso where unemployment runs fourteen percent. While he was there he drilled holes in polished rock for jewelry for a little while, but the holes were always off-center by a quarter of an inch. He dropped too many dishes on the Sambo's Restaurant job. Burger King told him he didn't have what it takes to be a Burger Boy. Fluorescent lights at Safeway were like strobes to him, made him disoriented and blind. He comes to be with me in the country just as the money is running out, and I am thinking it is time we all move to Dallas and get some jobs.

Leo doesn't want to go. He dreams of writing poetry about chickens and ducks the rest of his days, but knows as well as I do that some kind of money has got to be made. And no jobs in this little town we're living in, along the one downtown street all the boarded-up buildings only used to store sweet potatoes. The only people in the town, besides us, are either independent living on farm income or retired living on social security or young commuters traveling as much as one hundred twenty miles round trip to work every day. And that's not for me. Better to die from crime on the streets in Dallas than to live my life on the freeways, I say. Finally Leo acquiesces. He says he'll move to Dallas if I can find a place for less than two hundred a month, all bills paid. Then maybe we'll save up some money fast so we can move back to the country again (but it's a dream, isn't it Leo, I think but don't say, this country self-sufficiency, the two of us like awkward aliens in the midst of these smug farmers, who watch us serenely as our house peels its paint and our clothes give out).

I get a jump start for the truck from a mechanic down the road one Saturday morning, leave Leo with the tomatoes, leaning on his hoe like the farmer he isn't, his head full of tetrameter instead of compost and Sevin spray, and drive into Dallas with Morgani to find us a place, money in my pocket pooled by Leo, Morgani and me. I park the truck in East Dallas in front of the apartment of a jazz drummer friend whom I know doesn't have much money either. So I start walking up and down his street, the name of which is Swiss Avenue.

Now Swiss Avenue is a very special part of Dallas. It begins abruptly in the broken neighborhoods—vacant houses made rubble from the swaths carved out of them for access roads for North-Central Expressway cut just east of downtown. Then it curves past wooden hotels with weekly rates, liquor store/upholstery shop/broken glass across the sidewalks side by side with little clapboard houses still lived in by little granny women watering grass in the afternoons, who lock themselves inside wrought–iron barred doors at night with shotguns propped against TV sets and needlepoint in their laps. The street gets a little wider, more trees, the Public Immunization-For-The-Kids-And-Tetracycline-For-Herpes Clinic, the Dallas Theological Seminary, the apartments where the doughy seminarians hold prayer hours at night with their young pregnant wives, kneeling together on the shag carpet of the bedroom with iron grilles on the windows and iron gates across the courtyard doors locked at ten o'clock every night, and the other apartments with rock-and-roll blaring off the balconies where the Chicanos, Vietnamese men living off women waiting tables and hustling their asses, bikers, secretaries, black jazz drummers all live. Then no more than a mile and a half from where it began, the street suddenly widens into two lanes with a well-tended ribbon of city park in the middle, planted with flowers and trees. And the houses stop being apartments and become mansions, freshly renovated by young rich lawyers and bankers, only one family per house. There, where the street crests into wealth, rests the mansion of Brother Crumwell, whose congregation tends to wear suits Sunday mornings and sheets at night, a black holy smoke from kindled crosses heavy over downtown Dallas as carbon monoxide at eight o'clock rush, where his church spreads itself out for blocks just like he must have envisioned when he first founded it, the queen bee of the white Baptist churches in the antebellum South. And I think that the prayers of Brother Crumwell, a man strong enough to stare

55

his own dreams into stained glass and stone, directed at his downtown church and congregation from his mansion on Swiss Avenue two miles away, must be like a high-voltage tension line above the apartment buildings they pass over, jolting Baptists and seminarians and winos, racist landlords, and black tenants into an even wilder, stronger, longer, protonic-electronic dance, sizzling and sparking off each other in ecstatic revelation.

But I don't know much of this Saturday morning. All I know is that there are good old two-stories with ornate facades, twisted roots of very large trees breaking up the sidewalks just right, lots of squirrels. A FOR RENT sign springs suddenly into sight in front of a red-brick apartment house, $175.00 a month, shown by appointment only, it says, and just as suddenly I went to rent at this place, I want an appointment now, I am positive this is a cosmic sign, that the apartment will be just right. So I walk into the manager's apartment. There is a picture of Christ sweating blood while he prays at Gethsemane above the manager's desk, where a frizzy-haired woman is seated, long nosed, long mouth that wobbles around.

Oh, we say appointment only, she says, because we don't want to rent to niggers (she rolls her eyes) although they caught us just last week (she half whispers like there are ACLU lawyers in the hall listening to every word), they fined us through the apartment association, now we've even got one on the first floor. And oh-ho-ho, I think to myself, here is one of those, but I don't say anything, I don't defend my black brothers and sisters, I don't remind her that all of us born in the South like I was and she no doubt was, have plenty of off-the-record family ties, I don't command that herd of pigs living in her to come out. Instead I shuffle around, I look anywhere but at her in a terrible kind of pretense that I didn't really hear those words come out of her mouth, all because I want to live in her pretty little price-right apartment house. And then when she starts asking me questions, all this bullshit of my own starts spewing out. I don't tell her I am unemployed, I say I am a freelance writer working out of my own home, moving to Dallas to pick up some jobs with newspapers, the magazines, I show her a folded-up copy flat and worn I've been keeping in my wallet like an ID card of the only story I ever published with the *Dallas Morning News*: Ten Pointers on Buying Squash. Oh, you're a *writer*, she says, oh yes, I say, and my husband (*Doctor* Taylor) I say, used to work at the universities but he is tending right now to our country home and is a writer, also, and a poet like myself, anxious like I am to get a small Dallas apartment so that we can talk more intimately to all of these editors who have been wanting to see our work. Well, she says, writers would find this apartment house to be good for writing, quiet and nice. Shorty my husband who is really the landlord, not me, I just keep the key to the moneybox, she says, ha-ha, Shorty makes sure this apartment stays good and quiet. There may be these niggers and dirty greaseballs living in the apartments down the block playing their loud music, but Shorty is a good landlord, he doesn't let anyone rent who doesn't promise to be quiet, he makes everyone turn it down at ten o'clock. She herself, she says, reads poetry, there is poetry in *Guideposts* magazine, and she wonders if I have ever written anything for that. I say no, that I haven't seen that particular publication myself. Then she asks if I go to church and I tell her I used to go quite a lot, saying nothing about crazy holy rolling-in-the-aisles Pentecostal days before taking up marijuana pipes and sexual sweats again (the old hippie side of me too comfortably myself ever to die without returning). Her face lights up, Oh that's good, she says, have you found a church here yet? You should go with me and Shorty to ours sometime. It's the biggest one in the country, it's Brother Crumwell's Hard-Sell Baptist Church where Shorty is one of the elders. Yes, he used to be in prison but now he's an elder in the Hard-Sell Baptist Church and the landlord of twenty-eight apartment houses.

And of course, I think, Brother Crumwell is the name of this spirit that is making this woman flop her head around on her neck, squint her eyes and twist her mouth talking niggergreaseballdirtyanimalsmellofhippie Bible tells us do you go to church dear? Even living out of Dallas sixty miles I had heard some talk about Brother Crumwell. But I just keep on shuffling and smiling, not saying yes I'll go, or no, never, never, like hopeful tenants do to landlords everywhere, willing to disown children, lie about pets, and what kind of people they sleep with just to live at a decent price on a street with squirrels.

Just then a man stops in the doorway, looking at me like men look at old cars on sales lots trying to size up where they've been and how they've been driven. He has blue eyes and a broken front tooth, and because he's only five foot two, I figure this must be Shorty.

Oh, this is a writer, the woman says to him, I told her she didn't have to have an appointment, her husband and her need a city apartment to write in, they're tired of driving in all the time from their country home.

Gasoline prices, I tell him, everyone knows how that is.

He pulls out a key from his pocket and motions me down the hall. I only half-listen while he's telling me that he will be putting a new lock on the back door soon, that he keeps an eye on everyone coming and going, he doesn't let strangers wander in the halls, he runs a tight apartment house, he owns twenty-eight houses in the neighborhood, while he is opening one of the doors, while we are walking into this apartment and it is mine. It is mine! It is an efficiency, but an efficiency of grand style. A Murphy bed in the front room folds down from the wall, and there is a closet large enough for a little office if the clothes are pushed to the end of the rack. There is a kitchen and a space there for another desk behind the refrigerator, closet for me and kitchen for Leo, even though I am a little claustrophobic, better that Leo can look out the window and see trees than me, I don't mind. Then we can put a cot in the living room for Morgani and the three of us will be a little cozy. It's not exactly a townhouse, but will launch us in Dallas without taking all our money and I am in love with high ceilings and windows on two sides.

Now don't pay any attention to this fellow, Shorty waves to the door on the other side of the hall, he's a minister but he's a little off. He goes to church but they don't let him preach anymore.

We walk down the hall to the office. He knows I like his apartment, it doesn't matter if there's a Baptist across the hall or not. I tell him I talk to Baptist ministers all the time.

Back at the office Shorty ducks out for a minute when someone comes in the front door. Out in the hallway he starts talking about people who have friends who park in the wrong spaces in the parking lot. The wife has a long paper for me to sign. It's a six months' lease that says only two people living in an efficiency at a time, no pets, no children, a hundred-dollar deposit, all your belongings no longer yours if you don't pay the rent. Well, I don't know, I finally tell the long-mouthed wife, if this will work or not because there are my husband and myself, but there will also be Morgani, my eighteen-year-old son, living with us, at least until he gets a job. Oh well, she says, that will be all right. She hands me the ballpoint and I fill in Morgani's name on the lease agreement. It's not people like you we worry about, but you know the kind . . . Shorty comes in and looks at the lease agreement, now this Morgani, he says— oh that's her son, she says, he'll just be around till he gets a job. I give her one hundred and seventy-five dollars in small bills, then count out five more twenties for the deposit money, which she folds in a wad and sticks in a cashbox underneath the desk. We have these rules, Shorty says, about no more than two people to an efficiency, and he says, of course no pot in the rooms. We don't go for that.

We had a nigger girl come in just yesterday, the wife says, I could smell pot on her when she came in the door, and she had the nerve to lie about it when I told her we didn't go in for any of that.

For the first time I wonder if I have gone too far, overlooking too many potential danger signs in this landlord–tenant relationship, and maybe I should ask for my money back, take the lease form from the wife's hands where it is lying and tear it into pieces, but then I decide that I am as worthy of two walls of windows and a Murphy bed on Swiss Avenue as anyone else. Besides, I could always smuggle my clothes and TV set out one night if we had to leave in a hurry.

Oh our minister has such a good sense of humor, the wife says, you'd really love him. I nod and say I bet I would.

That afternoon I bring Morgani up to show him around. In the lobby we stop in front of the mailboxes where a long list of typewritten rules are posted in triplicate, one set to each wall, one inside the door, saying things like no washing cars in the parking lot, no loitering on the front lawn, no giving keys to friends, no leaving the back door open at night, no lights on in the laundry room, all violators being subject to getting thrown out. I point to number twelve, which has been typed in caps. That means that we only smoke grass in the walk-in closet with the door closed, I whisper in Morgani's ear, and you hide your bong when Shorty comes around. I walk him up the stairway, down the hall, get the key in the door just when the door on the opposite side opens and a pasty-faced man comes out. I certainly hope we'll get along with each other, he says, without any semblance of a smile. I can tell immediately that this must be the Baptist brother Shorty was talking about. Well, I certainly hope we get along with each other, too, I say, and we contemplate each other, eye to eye.

Well, I hope we won't be having any sort of problems, he says a little more pointedly.

I hope we won't have any sort of problems either, I tell him back, and then I know he is suddenly furious, it is inconceivable to him that I could imply a Baptist minister could give the same level of problems that a frizzy-haired woman accompanied by an eighteen-year-old long hair could give, so I slack off. I smile, well aren't these just wonderful apartments,

I gush. I am really looking forward to moving in, such great windows, such nice trees.

There are terrible cockroaches, he says.

Oh we're used to cockroaches, Morgani tells him.

And the noise is very bad, there is always noise, people going in and out, they never lock the back door either, and if you don't lock the back door, then Shorty will throw you out.

Well, I doubt we'll have any trouble with that, I say, opening the door, happy to know you, I say when Morgani and I are inside it. Morgani squints at me, growls his lip up and shows his teeth. I blow breath out. Morgani says I don't know about living here, and I say I don't know either, while I am pulling down the Murphy bed to show him. He says do you think I can play my guitar? And I say not through the amplifier. He goes over to the closet, maybe thinking that he can get some earphones and practice his guitar in there if he pushes all the clothes back, because I haven't told him yet that it will also have a writing desk, and while he looks around I bounce up and down once solidly on the Murphy mattress. The sun is coming through the oak trees outside the windows, and I am thinking that Leo, being a poet, will enjoy this palace of green and gold light. So I bounce up and down two or three more times, suddenly happy as any border smuggler when suitcases are safely opened after contraband has crossed the line.

▲▲▲▲▲▲

WHO'S
THAT
KNOCKING?
IS
IT
YOU?

Once the storm comes up
and the image of Christ appears
when the Devil jumps through your window
and you see the Virgin Mary weep real tears
will you stay in the same apartment?
will you continue selling Mason shoes?
oh Lord I am down on my knees
in the plaza with the winos
I've got the total transformation blues . . .

—*fr.* Pentecostal Patty's Songbag of
Used-Up Testaments & Paid Dues

Winchell's Donuts is one block over from our apartment house and four blocks down, a good place for everyone in the neighborhood to hang out, black, Chicano, Anglo dropout boys taking turns at the classifieds left on the unsteady little orange disc stools grafted onto the tables like plastic school desks, reading the ads under Miscellaneous Employment and Used Cars from noon until suppertime. And the street girls after that, just waking up when the pavement's cooling off, coming in for a couple of peanut-topped strawberry glazed creme-filled plain sugar and coffee to go, eating them out of the paper wraps, licking their fingers, waving little fannies in red sateen and hefty fannies in wide white hot pants at the Winchell's clientele on their way out the door.

Leo goes down to Winchell's to drink coffee and get out of the efficiency apartment that grows too small for three people fast. He reads about anarchy and talks to the Winchell's street-intellectual league, he comes home one night telling me about two men he met, one who does janitor work at the Catholic church several blocks down where the illegal alien kids are taught illegal English classes in the basement, and one named Judas who is an ex-Child of God. The janitor had been reading W. G. Wedgewood's *Tudor and Stuart Poetry* when Leo walked in, a book Leo thought only graduate English students ever read, but there you are, the janitor said he had bought it at a garage sale because it was only a quarter and looked like fun. They talked about poetry a little and Tudors a little and then moved onto God when Judas heard them talking and sat down with his coffee, a Bible in his coat pocket. The three of them talked loudly until closing time.

You would like to talk to this Judas, Leo tells me while he climbs in on his side of the Murphy bed, son Morgani not asleep yet on the couch, he knows a place to sleep for five dollars a week, he's been arrested for panhandling in Highland Park. Leo tells me all he can remember that Judas said about St. Paul and women and who the seven-headed beast will be. Leo tried to report all religious conversations he engages in because he knows that sometime before he met me

I was supposed to have gotten a little bit crazy about Jesus Christ. I always tell him that was a stage, something that happens for a time to some women when they aren't making enough love during their sexual practices, and then sometimes I tell him well, I was just hanging out with Jesus until the right man came along, someone bearded and skinny with love of the word more than love of money, who would also screw a lot. Still, when Leo begins to say that he said this and Judas said that, I begin to make bad paraphrases of scripture and try to remember what books and chapters they come from, looking at Leo in the dark with my eyes wide open, perfectly solemn about what I am saying until he is asleep and I am still awake, finally quiet after I realize I have talked too much. And I think that having gone a little crazy once for Jesus is like having scar tissue left from a hot love affair. There is a ganglia of nerves somewhere along the spinal column, lines of body feeling fused and cauterized where they once converged after leaping simultaneously, making a lightning bridge to meet the rain of fire. And certain combinations of sounds hit those scar ridges just right so that little bits of Matthew Mark Luke and John start tumbling out.

The next day on our way to buy a six-pack Leo points out an apartment building with rotted-out timbers across the porch steps, windows with no glass, a half-open front door, useless padlock hanging by a nail. That's the place Judas has been sleeping in, he says. Five dollars a week, four or five men in a room sleeping on the floor. We walk on by and I can see just a little of the paper-stripped wood on an inside wall through a street-level window. Imagine the men asleep together on the floor, the scurrying, rustling snores and groans and cries, mingled smells—sickness vomit urine and booze—they must all share at night. It is amazing to me that I have walked by this place before, thinking it was empty and uninhabitable, never once realizing that its rooms were filled.

A few nights later we walk to Tom Thumb Supermarket for bread and longhorn cheese and there is a small man with pants too long for him, a black suitcoat with sleeves over his hands, a plentiful beard.

Judas? Leo says. The man turns and squints at us. Is that Leo? he asks.

How are you doing? Leo claps him on the shoulder, this is my wife, he says, that I was telling you about.

When Judas turns to me I can see that he is younger than I am, hardly thirty, with good blue eyes and a good smile even though his hair is dirty, combed straight back in flat thin ribbons behind his ears and over the suitcoat collar, which is folded up on one side.

I decide not to say much, better not to say Leo's been telling me all about you or any of that crap, so Leo and he talk a little about something, the price of longhorn cheese or how hard it is to carry a bunch of groceries home from Tom Thumb since they switched from paper bags to plastic. Then Leo says listen, why don't you come home with us for a cup of coffee, so I say *really,* like I have heard wifey-hostesses say all my life, and there is a flash of some kind of remembering across Judas's face that when people are being social this is the kind of thing they say and do. He looks from Leo to me fast, his near-sight under squinted-up eyebrows seeing something that looks all right, so we walk back to the apartment, Leo in the middle, me not really listening. And I am thinking, recollecting, wondering about that old Brother Bob, if he ever started playing the piano again after God told him it was too much vanity, and if he still has the revival tent he bought from the piano sale. And I wonder about Brother John, if he is still running the orphanage in Zaragosa with his street preacher wife from Mexico and if they ever got it straightened out between them whether or not women could instruct men or if preaching wives could only preach to other women. And then I wonder about Brother David and Brother Mack for a while before I realize that I am wondering about all the religious men I have known, putting them in a major category like that, and then adding Judas. So here, I am thinking, is another religious man. I listen to his voice a little bit talking to Leo and like the slow straight way he has of speaking, all true tones. And then I think this Judas is somewhat attractive even though he is down-and-out, something still fiery in all these men who really try to be religious, fasting and praying and trying to take St. Paul's advice about women to heart, something that makes me think when one of them does come in a woman, it must be like getting screwed with a loose power wire. But then too many of them begin to hallucinate, have blurred vision from their bodies not getting enough of just about everything, and that's why a wise woman will keep aware when she finds herself alone at night with an overly religious man, as the present moment they are sharing can suddenly dichotomize for him into the world he wishes to attain and the world he wishes to shun, and the unwary woman might find herself hacked to pieces when he starts separating his life into two piles.

At home I go to the kitchen to make instant coffee. Leo is saying to Judas this is Morgani, my stepson. Morgani with punk-purple hair steps back into the closet after the briefest hello, his battery-charged headphone amplifier hooked into his electric guitar with the door closed for the rest of the night. Morgani knows this is Judas calling from the way Leo told the Winchell's Donuts story, but he's seen too much of the religiously crazy himself, mother once crying crazy kneeling in the aisles, crazy preacher uncle converted hippie, crazy Jesus Christ aunt praying that his eyes may be healed although they never are, he becomes a musician instead before his mother brings Leo home and stops reading the Bible at night. I watch the teakettle while it heats up, thinking that I won't go into the living room, I'll let Leo and Judas talk, I'll take advantage of the little social dance some women learn to do early, keeping to themselves while the men talk, doing things at the kitchen sink, closing the living room door, but then I think no that wouldn't be kind . . . to treat a guest . . . Leo bringing his friend home . . . a little social conversation . . .

So I carry three cups of coffee to the living room, put one cup in front of Leo, one in front of Judas, sit down on the floor with mine because there are no chairs, only the couch that Judas and Leo are sitting on. I try one of those polite questions. I say, Leo tells me that you are an ex-Child of God.

Judas puts down his cup of coffee right away, frowns into the top of it, nods his head up and down.

Didn't something happen to Moses whats-his name, that Child of God leader, Leo asks, good casual conversation. Didn't he get a little strange, didn't he get too interested in screwing around?

Oh yes, Judas swinging around to Leo, there was sex all the time, everybody all the time into that.

Well, I say.

Except for me, Judas says, takes a sip again on his coffee not too serious about it after all.

Oh well, I say.

I had to pray about it all the time. But the truth is, he says, shifting his coffee mug on his lap, no woman likes to look at my dick, it was maimed in an accident.

I don't ask what happened, I don't say anything, I keep on looking at him nod his head, caught in a little pleasant social smile.

I was in a mental institution, he says, there was homosexual rape if you know what I'm talking about, I don't remember everything, electric shock, I don't remember what the people looked like, now I probably see them every day, sometimes I do see one that I think I remember but I can't be sure because the shock confused me, I have a lot blanked out, but when I finally began waking up it had already happened, I had been the subject of a terribly perverted experiment, so now, he makes a vague pass of his hand over his lap, all of this is messed up. He sips his coffee, gives his head a little shake, like: it's a sad story all right but what else can I say?

I wonder what his penis looks like, I imagine something like a mangle-headed club. Leo's mouth is open but he has no words. How did you wind up in the mental institution, I finally say.

Judas holds up one hand. There are two fingers missing, the two middle ones, small stumps from the first knuckle up splayed red. I did this to myself with a hatchet, he says.

I guess that would do it, I say. It sure would, Leo says. Judas laughs, we all laugh like it's a funny joke, yes it sure did, he says.

He tells me it is very good coffee, by the way. I ask him where he works and he says he is mowing lawns. We say some other things, Leo shows him some photographs, we move into the kitchen where Judas sits straight in a straight-backed chair, me washing dishes, looking at the soapsuds, copping out. Judas takes a wadded-up piece of white bread out of his pocket.

I always carry some bread with me, he says. He picks off some of the crust and puts it in his mouth. The Lord said eat of this bread and think of me, so I always feel better because of carrying this around. You might just try it yourself, he says, holding up the leftover pieces for me to see at the sink, then you can just take it out whenever you feel like it and have a little bit.

He gives a piece to Leo who puts a little in his mouth, concentrates on its white Wonder-bread taste and Judas's pants pocket smell. It tastes all right, he says, good TV commercial voice praising instant communion, hands the rest back to Judas who holds it in the three-fingered hand. See this? pointing down to the stumps again, I was cutting wood with a circular saw one time, there was just one little slip and those had had it. He smiles and shrugs his shoulders: it's sad to lose some fingers to an unhappy accident, but what can you say?

He finally gets up to leave. I want you to know, he says, that this is the first time in years that I have been in someone else's house. Well, he says, I've been in other people's houses some but not like this, to visit, and I felt that it was right. Well, he says, I felt that it was almost right. Leo pats his shoulder. You should just drop by again whenever you feel like it, he says. Yes you should, I say, maybe not with the proper sincerity but close, Judas cocking his head to pick up all the off-vibrations.

Maybe I will he says, or well, for sure I'll pray about it, I'll ask the Lord about it.

If the Lord says it's right, Leo says.

That's right, Judas says.

We'll just have to see, I say.

Well, we say, good night, good night, good night.

Morgani comes out of the closet. My God, Leo, he says, why did you bring him home?

Now Morgani, I say, he is an interesting man.

His name is Judas and he is an ex-Child of God.

Well, of course that does sound a little crazy, I say.

Of course it *is* crazy, Morgani stating the obvious because he is still young, only eighteen years old.

Well, Leo says later when the Murphy bed is unfolded and the lights are out, the light from the hallway only a sharp edge beneath the door, don't ever open the door for him if I'm not here.

Oh don't worry, I say, lying on my stomach, clutching the pillow, my eyes open, thinking what I would tell Judas, what would I say if he came to the door knocking and Leo was gone, would I forget all pretense then of being his friend, the slice of light under the door big enough so that I could see his shoes if they were standing outside, thinking that maybe Judas's dick is not maimed, maybe it is simply a dick that has erections that he believes women see as being ugly, which, in fact, some women do. So he has had some bad experiences, he has been too sensitive to some young girl's recoiling, he has looked too closely when some young virgin eyed his first hard-on, but usually there is Morgani in the apartment at night always asleep on the couch, practicing his guitar at home when Leo is gone, and it could be that Judas is really maimed, bad things happen to people, terrible things. How young was he, I wonder, when he became a Child of God, on and on thinking about Judas, turned on my side, staring at the bottom of the door as the light in the hall continues shining.

69

AFOOT
IN
A
FIELD
OF
MEN

I have been a secretary these last few weeks, a job I said I'd never take again, a person I believed I wasn't anymore. But it is temporary work, it is Kelly Girl, queen bee of temporaries, offices two dozen floors above the trees with plush carpets, glass tables, and oriental palms. And when I sit down on the waiting room couch my day of testing and application, I remember why the first time, when I was just married, first babied and wanting money, that I had lost myself in the Land of the Offices so long. It is very quiet, you see, there is Muzak and the clicking away of typewriters, all the women wear little-bitty high-heeled shoes and tiptoe around. The grey desks are isolated in their cubicles, the secretaries turned from the doors, fingers playing over the typewriter keys as they dream into the walls above them day after day, the rush of poppy buds unfolding through the earwires of the dicta-phones. As I wait for the results of my typing test, the vines twine toward me from an artful planter by the couch, I leaf through old *Vogues* and nibble on a cookie that Kelly Girls set out on a silvery tray. A woman tiptoes up to me in her tippy-toe high heels and smiles down. She has gold-blond hair in a braid looped around her head, Rapunzel's great-granddaughter in a silk suit coat and pearl-drop earrings. She tells me I am a wonderful typist and that I can be a Kelly Girl, too, beginning at five dollars and thirty-five cents an hour. Money and Muzak and quiet tippy-toeing women to hang around with all day. Better than sitting at home, like I did last year, cooking pots of beans, trying to write the story of every-thing, waiting for the money to run out, which it always does for me in a quick, quiet and inevitable way. Besides, it is temporary, after all. I am not going to work too long.

So I go to work on January second, all the regular secretaries in Dallas staying late at the New Mexico ski resorts with their lovers, suffering from postholiday depressions, call-ing in sick with the flu. I am to work at Henry S. Miller Inc. I suppose Henry Miller was once a man who grew offices and buildings, warehouses and residential homes onto himself like some people grow seed warts, a real estate firm that buys and sells huge chunks of Dallas and Houston, with a list of over-seas offices like a two-week special European tour painted on the front door. I don't know if the original Henry Miller is still alive or if I am delivering memos and typing reports in the halls and spaces of some gigantic sloughed-off outer form, perpetually preserved with cash flow. The men I see are uni-dentified to me and look the same, slipping in and out of their offices in white shirts and dark suits with prim ties like men have worn for the past hundred years. No doubt they are all *somewhat* Henry Miller. I wait, as I am told to do by the

71

woman in charge of paperwork, until the men are out of their offices to slip in and put fresh-typed letters in their in-files and pick up dictaphone tapes from their out-files, part of an illusion that their words bloom magically into substance on paper formed from air. Then I listen all afternoon to their compositions, copying every word down, my whole body turned into the little earplugs like the prophets must have listened before writing down the books of the Bible and like the shotgun madmen listen today to the UFO voices from the other side of the moon.

After a week the errant secretaries drift back in, and I go to work for an architectural firm housed in the top floor of the tallest building in Dallas. The secretaries are put into little cubicle boxes in the center of the office space and the architects are ranged along the outside walls, each with a window from ceiling to floor, so that the old ones can look out and pat their stomachs at buildings erected from the specifications of their most virile dreams, and the young ones can dream demolitions of the penile forests to make way for something even taller (taller than the Hyatt-Regency! domes! spires! revolving balls!). The men meet every day in a large conference room with chairbacks as high as thrones around a polished table with inlaid wood, back clapping, asking about the Dallas Cowboys games, being straightforward with each other (give it to me straight, they say, and don't give me that bullshit, Bert . . .). The secretaries bustle along the sideboard, bringing trays of donuts in the mornings, pouring coffee into styrofoam cups, asking that age-old question: cream or sugar? one man at a time. Once the serving is complete, the secretaries tiptoe out, close the doors. Nothing interrupts the masculine convention until noon when the sandwiches come. When the meeting breaks up and the men catch their planes back to New York or Houston, or go to happy hour with each other or do a little desk work until quitting time, the secretaries divide up the remaining donuts and eat them with late afternoon coffee. They are still very good even though the sugar gets crunchy and the texture tough by then. I have just taken to prowling around the closed conference doors in the afternoons, hoping to be first at the leftover donuts, hoping to get maybe a peanut crunchy instead of a plain, when the secretary I am replacing comes back to her desk, married and honeymooned in two short weeks, a pleasant enough interlude but ready to be back at work again.

Finally I find myself in the thick of sales, out of the downtown offices into the new office space complexes along streets called Regal Row, Viceroy Way, Executive Circle, President Avenue, tickling the ambitions of the tenants and adding subliminal content to their letterheads. The president of the firm is not as aloof as the real estate men and architects have been. He has come from a farm in Arkansas to the city, where he has learned to sell Muzak sound systems so well that now, less than forty years old, he is the owner of a sound systems sales company himself. A bouncy, athletic man with sculptured sideburns, he claps his hand down on his desk periodically and sings out to me through his half-opened door to my outer office, Are we making money, Pat, or are we making money? Then I stop typing, turn around in my chair to face him, smile and say we are certainly making money! He begins to like me very much for my ability to do this so well and keeps me working even after a new secretary is hired.

Now this particular secretary, whom I shall call Betty Lee, a good small-town East Texas name because that is where she is originally from, is in love with a male go-go-dancer called the Macho Man who strips every Thursday, Friday and Saturday night at La Bare. I have heard about La Bare before. I know that men dance on tables for women who tuck dollar bills under the elastic g-strings of the men whose bulges and bumps they approve of. But I have never gone and when Betty hears this, she promises that someday soon, after work, she will take me. Now it really isn't for me, I don't have to have that kind of vicarious experience. After all, I have never even liked bars too much, I am not interested in seeing half-naked men dance on the tables, I think women who go to La Bare, in fact, must be a little insane. But Betty brings out in me a feminine archetype that I have only viewed (and loathed) before in other women: I begin to wriggle, my wrists get limper, my eyes begin to roll around, and I agree with everything she says in exclamation points (you don't mean it, girl! now that's the truth! that's amazing/incredible/fantastic/bizarre!). So when Betty promises to take me to La Bare, only a small part of me looks on in contempt and mourning for my own integrity, buzzing on about female sin and dissimulation, while the material side of myself claps and whistles, smirks and nods. Betty assures me I'll never recover. Of course, I agree.

In the meantime I learn some things about Betty. Right now it is February, and it was only last August that she split with a man. She still isn't quite divorced. The divorce has two or three weeks of paperwork or waiting time or whatever to go. And her husband was a shithead, he was a redneck, unkind, untrue, unkempt, uninteresting. He watched football games and never kept her company. They dated for five years and then they got married and they never were happy. They were married for two years before they broke up.

The Macho Man, on the other hand, is Dallas while her husband was only Small Texas Town. The Macho Man has a beard and an all-leather outfit. He wears a leather strap around his neck and some leather straps up and down his arms, and Betty points to her own body to show where those straps are. After she does, she wiggles on her chair a little, rolls her eyes up to the ceiling, and putting her top teeth over her bottom lip, makes an inverted whistle. This is a traditionally female signal that means *sensually overwhelmed*. I myself say wow wow wow, in order to show that I am no intellectual snob, that I, too, am no slouch when it comes to imagining all of those leather straps on that bearded man.

One days she gets a photobutton out of her purse. You want to see him, she asks. I gave him a ten-dollar tip last night and he gave me this photobutton. I take it in my hand

and look at it for that particular length of time I have learned is good when being shown photos of children or lovers, which is as long as possible while maintaining a steady flow of flattering remarks and different flattering gestures with the mouth and eyes. Wow, I say, he sure is cute, I do like men with beards, my husband has a beard, too. He's called Macho Man? (I intermittently shake my head back and forth as though Macho Man's looks are just beyond me to describe.) Finally she takes the button from my hand, obviously pleased with the ninety-second show. So I say, well, why don't you pin it on your shirt? She says maybe she shouldn't and I egg her on a little, so she does and wears it the rest of the day. The boss doesn't say anything. The foreman comes in with a ticket for Muzak speakers, what's that, he asks, staring at her left breast where the photobutton is pinned. That's Macho Man, she says, the breast swelling up a little to show him off. The foreman doesn't put his head any closer but squinting, says oh, hazards no further questions, walks away.

Another day she comes in flushed and excited. There is something she has been wanting to tell me since it happened the night before. This is the thing, in fact, she wants to tell as many people as she possibly can, because her mind is choke full of it, her mind can't think of anything else. The next day is her birthday. She is going to be twenty-seven years old. And the Macho Man is coming to her party. The Macho Man is coming to her party? Incredible! He is coming to her birthday party. I wrote him a note last night, she says, I told him I am having a birthday party and asked if he would like to come. Really, she says, it was an afterthought. I thought he would say no. But he said (and she pauses for effect)—when and what time? When and what time! So I'm counting the hours. Oh I swear, girl, I can't wait! I just can't wait! Betty is giving little shivers and bridling like a nervous horse, smoking a cigarette and fanning herself with the smoke. She is just nobody Betty Lee, but she has a date for her birthday with Macho Man.

Now Betty is not a very pretty woman, she tries too

hard to make up for that. She puts cheekbone rouge all the way up her temples, and for eyebrows she draws little lines so high up she looks a little startled all the time. I try to imagine how she would look if she had long brown hair parted in the middle instead of the little flappy short-trimmed secretary style that she has. I try to imagine her own natural face framed in the hair, with its pulpy kind of nose and long solemn chin, and she doesn't look bad that way at all. But even that way, given long dream hair and perched on a dream horse, all rosewater nude clutching daisies, she does not seem to look like the kind of woman the Macho Man would go for. But who am I to say? So I make entries in the ledger columns in the hundreds and thousands of dollars for Muzak sound systems multiplying the romantic Mantovani strings in office cubicles just like ours a million times, while Betty Lee goes on and on and on.

This is what is supposed to happen on her birthday. First she is going to come to work. She is going to bring a dress and curling iron and some makeup, so she can change and be ready to go right after work.

I happen to like myself in this color, she says. She is just a little shy about saying that, nods her head and puts both palms against the dark green material stretched over her chest, so I bought a dress just about this color, except that it's strapless *and*—she sticks out her leg and measures—it's slit up to here on both sides. I ogle, say wow.

So after putting this incredibly indecent dark green dress on, and curling her hair up into devastating flips and giving just a little more tone and depth to various facial dips and curves, she is going to jump into her Camaro and drive it to a well-known lounge where she will meet four men and a woman from a firm where she used to work, all of whom are just ordinary people, as well as Mr. Macho Man, who will be Mr. Everything-There-Is. And she won't take them to any singles bars, because she doesn't want women asking the Macho Man to dance.

He asked me what I wanted to do for my birthday, she

76

says, and I told him you're going to take me out dancing! Aw, he said, I dance for a living—Ha! I say to the predictable line—and I said you'll like to dance with me! Hmmmmm, I say, grinning and winking and clucking, letting her spin on.

So they will have dinner first, and then they will dance, and then—It is too much, too soon, too early, too dangerous, too breathtaking to even begin to imagine. She rolls her eyes back and takes a deep breath and lights a cigarette when she comes too close to touching on the verbalization of that—? Still there it is. The truth is that he said he was coming two or three times. Six o'clock at the lounge at the Holiday Inn? he asked me. Six o'clock I said. Oh shiver and roll, we sit there and shake at each other, she ravished with the joy of telling, me tiring but still cheerful with the chore of listening, locked into that sweet copulation only the ear and mouth can do.

The day of her birthday she does indeed come with her dress, curling iron and makeup. And she is nervous to the point of sickness. She is pale, she is smoking a lot of cigarettes, she can't quite get her breath, and her eyes, as the morning progresses, tend to roll up even more than usual, as she flutters on the very edge of breakdown at the possibility that her dream of Macho Man may become real. She asks me to pat her hand for reassurance and I think, my God, this has gone too far! Patting Betty Lee's hand in this circumstance is a disgusting act, and Betty is a disgusting twit and deserves to faint at her Muzak receptionist desk with her dictaphone plug wired into her head. But the word *twit* sets up some strange mantralike vibration in my head, flashing terrible obscene images of myself as a twit, yearning and cowlike in scene after half-forgotten scene over any number of incompatible men, so that I stop thinking twit fast, yes yes, I'm a twit, too, Betty Lee. So I pat her hand and she squeezes my hand and I pat her hand some more, as much as she wants, on and off all day. By the afternoon Betty is oblivious, she is half dead from the wait of five and four and three hours more. But finally at five o'clock she is squeezing my hand one last time, looking deeply into my eyes, asking me to wish her luck, which of course I do, and I go out to wait for the bus to come, reading the *Times-Herald* headlines through the wire cage at the bus stop instead of paying money, wondering mildly what story I am going to be listening to from Betty Lee the next day.

As any story-listener will suspect, it isn't a good one. Betty Lee is crying all the next day. There had been a birthday party, four people from her other place of work, but Macho Man had never shown up. She goes from her desk to the women's room and back with handfuls of soggy toilet paper. She has to answer the phone half a dozen times and tell people she has talked to the day before that Macho Man hadn't come after all. He didn't come, he didn't come, he didn't come. She says it over and over.

I'm going to the country this weekend with another man, she says, I've got to get away from this, he's driving me crazy, I'm not going to La Bare anymore, he's driving me out of my mind.

I agree. She is right to get away, La Bare is too much money for her budget, Macho Man is too much leather for her head. She cries and I handle her telephone while she stays in the bathroom, the boss glowering but philosophical. He's had soggy secretaries, it has something to do with the menstrual cycle, he is sure, he can put up with this crying thing, just so long as they come to work. By three o'clock Betty Lee remembers she doesn't have enough money to go to the country and besides it's my last day, isn't it? I tell her that it is, the next day I'll be back to the tall buildings downtown. So she still hasn't taken me to La Bare like she promised, she says, yes, she really should take me, I should at least see the place, just have one drink at happy hour, Macho Man won't even be working then. And I protest, she doesn't need to, she shouldn't go, but she insists, her face puffy but her cigarette steady, after all, she had said before this happened (or didn't happen) that she would take me, she can't go back on her word.

So at six o'clock in the heat of happy hour I am finally
there, in a dark two-tiered bar with a runway surrounded by
women just off from work packed around every little table, all
ages, all sizes, laughing and drinking through a sorority celebration of their own. Betty Lee picks out a good table, orders
me a two-dollar wine. The music is up, the emcee is on, and
the men dance up and down the runway with very little on,
except for tiny sequined bags holding the limp parts of themselves, flopping up and down to the music. Then at certain
times Mr. Dynamo or the Prince or Mr. Gyration dances off
the runway and onto the tops of tables where women squeal
and clap and shout and stick lots of dollars into the g-strings.

Listen, I tell Betty Lee, shouting to be heard over the
sound, you're an attractive woman. You're very young yet. It's
too soon after your divorce anyway to be thinking about men.
Wait and see what kind of person you are first. I know. I
remember how it all was myself.

But the disco sound system drowns all my good advice
out and the Prince has begun to dance on our table. I study
his ankles, which are shapely in their high stretch up and
down, and the blonde hair that begins on his toes and goes
up his legs as far as I want to follow it. Betty leans back in her
chair so that she can see his face better. Where's Macho Man
tonight? she asks.

The Prince rolls his arms around each other and
thrusts his little bag out toward her side of the table. He'll be
in later, he says.

She smiles and takes sips from her drink and we don't
try to talk to each other anymore for a while, we just watch
the Prince's feet and ankles and other moving parts through
his dance, his g-string filling up with dollar bills.

▲▲▲▲▲▲

BIRD
PRAYER
AND
NO
AMEN

Winter in Dallas. Leo, Morgani and me tucked into the efficiency apartment, couch and folded Murphy bed like two islands of unmade sheets and quilts floating in a sea of old newspapers, Winchell's coffee cups, beer cans, plates, forks, spoons—all styrofoam—of various sizes, shorts, socks, pools of shirts, skirts, panties, blouses, towels nobody hangs up after, small black television everyone spends a lot of time in the evenings looking at. Leo drinks generic beer. Morgani and I smoke marijuana sitting together on my writing desk in the walk-in closet so the smoke won't blow out of the living

room vent into the hallway where Shorty might catch a sniff
and call the cops, and so enforce landlord rule number
twelve: POT-SMOKERS GET THEMSELVES THROWN OUT.

Inside the building Shorty patrols the hallways, making sure tenants are keeping their radios and televisions
turned down and their doors locked. But outside the front
door and past the square brown lawn Shorty's straight Baptist
rule disintegrates, as the block runs to shiny black Chicano
low-riders and Jesus-freak vans with holy fire painted in orange running off the front fenders, gunshots at night and
sirens in the alley behind the supermarket, taxi driver asking
on the corner have you seen that blonde hooker that's always
here, flat brown bottles on the sidewalk when I walk to work
past the park in the morning, everybody asking me Are you
sure you should be walking to work through that neighborhood?

We're all working. In the morning everyone up at
six-thirty, Morgani into the bathtub, blow-drying purple
punked-out hair, red suspenders, grey corduroys for the carwash. He catches the Abrams-Mockingbird bus but still has
to walk two miles at the end of the line. Leo and me work
Kelly Girl, Leo bumming out fast from so much joking
around—Leo the Kelly Girl, Leo the poet, Leo the man who
comes home and watches TV with a quart of beer at night
completely wiped out.

And me, walking along the downtown sidewalks, underneath the North-Central Expressway, past the liquor store
where black men wave brown packages out, say Don't you
talk to black men, *huh?* thinking about when I used to live in
the desert, when I'm going to be rich, when I won't have to
be a Kelly Girl anymore, when I'm going to tell just the right
story, it's going to come to me, and it's going to be the right
story to get me out of here, walking back past the park where
the winos come at night and pool their money to buy the
bottles they line the gutters with once they're emptied.

In the later afternoon the birds come before the
winos, hundreds of blackbirds, grackles, swirling over the

park, resting in the tops of the trees like large black leaves come to cover the bare branches, the sidewalks white with grackle guano, and here and there in the grass the dead stiff body of a grackle, died in his sleep waiting for the spring to come before following the wind on to Kansas and Illinois and wheat fields coming ripe all the grackles dream about. After dark the winos will come, grackles and winos occupying the roots and branches each to his own, watching the moon in its phases barely clearing the Dallas skyline.

Before Grackle Park, I am always walking along the sidewalk thinking about everything. But when I get to the park, at half past five and the sky is turning red and grey and the grackles are flying down into the branches, finding each other, making the hiss-whizz-crack-and-cackle hundreds of times, I stop thinking about everything except grackles and grackles, my head filled with them like one of the trees. One day I stop in the middle of the sidewalk. I think that I will try and call to one of the grackles with my mind. I will call out Come to me, come to me, come to me, and I will try to think of the motion, of a grackle flying through the air and landing on my shoulder. So I pick out a bird by himself at the top of a very tall tree. I look at him squarely and think as loudly as I can Come to me, come to me, trying to concentrate on the motion. But he continues to sit, looking in the sky, in the branches, at the other birds, never at me, so the energy is gone and I stop thinking at him and continue walking along the whitened sidewalk, the litter of dead birds and leaves along the gutter and the swirl of birds still coming down from the sky. And blocks away from Grackle Park, I forget the birds completely, wondering if Morgani scored roaches from the ashtrays at the carwash, wondering if I should go to the laundromat so that I'll have something clean to wear for work tomorrow, wondering what to make for supper.

▲▲▲▲▲▲

ANSWERING
THE
INQUISITOR

Ira.

Ira opens his door when Morgani is carrying a guitar case out of ours.

Are you a musician, he asks. Is that a guitar? Why all this going and coming at night, he asks. Why are you always opening and closing that downstairs door?

Ira is pasty and sluggish and round. I put these adjectives in a string that way because I don't like him. He lives by himself and listens to the cars come in and out of the parking lot at night, always reading his Bible praying so loudly

I can hear him from across the hall. I don't like his loneliness that makes him seem to be a crazy man, capable of anything in the name of God.

Morgani says Bullshit and Listen man, puts one shoulder up and squints at him a little to focus.

I come out of the apartment. Is there a problem? I ask him, taking care of this encounter between neighbor and son as my good-given backbone unfurls like a cobra fan and I meet his marbly stone-bone eyes with mine four-square head-on.

There's bound to be some kind of a problem, Ira says, when people are going in and out all the time.

Ira knows. He sees young women living only doors down from his who let young men in and out of those doors to spend afternoons spreading legs wide in beds, in bathtubs, up and down over kitchen chairs, oh he knows it all, he can well imagine what is going on. And he sees this teenaged boy coming in and out of the apartment across from his own, who says I am his mother even though there are too many names on the mailbox, even though there is a man with a beard who lives in the apartment, too, and then there are men and women, too, knocking, going in and out. He can really very well imagine what is going on.

I think you wouldn't like Ira. If you were living in my apartment with an adolescent son and bearded poet-lover you might come out in the hallway, too, when Ira is talking. You might say what I refrain from saying, that Ira's loud voice calling the demons out of the hearts of his neighbors is at least as disturbing as the door opening and closing when people come in and out. A young woman down the hall comes out of her apartment when she hears us talking and says something to that effect herself. Morgani agrees, encouraged. So I agree, too, the three of us nodding, arms crossed in the apartment hall, telling him his voice is too loud.

You have too many secrets, he says while he points his finger, you need to examine your heart. There is salvation, he says, there is sin there is sexchrist demon demption redemp-

tion in the holy eyes of the lamb. But I know that language,
I've been to church before, so I counter his words. Holy ghost,
I say to him, praise GodalmightyJesus Christsavior. You are
a bully and I have Christ himself living with me in my apartment, yes, I need him every day to be able to handle you.

You are the devil, he says. He tries to penetrate with
his eyes.

No, I say, *you* are the devil. The conversation degener-
ates from there. Ira slams his door. Morgani heads back out.
I go back in. My lover has gone out to work and will come
in later.

Robert Mitchum played a Baptist minister several
years ago in a film set in the South. He was searching the
swamps for children to kill while singing *Bringing in the sheaves,
bringing in the sheaves*. It becomes late, and Morgani is still out.
I have promised myself I won't open my door if there is a
knock. If there is a knock, I will ask, who is it? And if he says,
Ira, I just won't come out. I think you will probably agree with
me that this is wise.

Flannery O'Conner made her ministers wild men.
They were charlatans and pretended to throw acid on themselves. A woman in the newspaper yesterday was accused of
roasting a baby to get the demons out of it.

I had planned to write an essay on sex with animals
this evening. I was going to explain to you why it is taboo.
Goats really dance to flutes, I am told, if the flute player is any
good. Turkeys sing to flutes, too. But Ira has been to church
tonight and now is coming in the door downstairs. These
typewriter keys tap out code through the walls that he trans-
lates with an instinct learned hundreds of years ago. Now his
key rattles across the hall. He is speaking very quietly but I
can hear the question he is asking me, the same question he
asks all the time, which is if I am indeed a musician, like my
son. So I play my typewriter keys now in answer, so that he
can hear Morgani whistling in the hall coming home after
work, so that he can see me riding the stairs looking for my
bearded lover wondering when he's coming in, so that he can

hear the chorus singing through the apartment walls like the Bremen musicians singing together, roosters singing to the dancing goats, singing oh remember, Ira, dear Ira (these are the words of our song), the shepherd who looks after the flock best eats them up later on, singing even while I type these words out, and Ira's praying from across the hall goes on and on.

ACQUIRING
POINT
OF
VIEW

There is an old woman I know who lives alone in the desert. When I talk about her I call her wise, I tell people she is eighty years old, that she lives with goats, that rumor has it she can heal people by simply using her hands. And suddenly it is springtime, I am saying this about the woman to publishers and that about contracts, and maybe I will write this all up, I am saying, and I will even print this my-self, swaggering around in the apartment, talking fast and loud to anyone who will listen—oh, there will be a meeting with this woman in the desert, I will bring champagne, I will make arrangements, get money, so many telephone calls to make and receive. At the same time Leo becomes disheartened. He says there are not enough windows in the apartment, there are not enough rooms or beds. And he wants to leave me, he has told all our friends, I can hear it in their voices both solicitous and curious on the telephone. So when he leaves me alone one evening at the apartment, closing the door without saying if he will be back, I sit down in a chair in front of the television feeling too large and heavy and awkward for anyone to want to live around long. Besides, there is no money, no Kelly Girl check that was supposed to come, and there is no grass, not even seeds or roaches, and there is no Morgani, he is at a movie or a punk rock club, gone somewhere leaving me alone, alone, alone.

So the more I rock back in the chair, watching the little brown cockroaches roam around the Cheerios box above the television picture that is fast becoming a black and white blur, the sadder I feel, the more loaded and heavy with responsibility. I think that I have taken on too many people to care for and that I won't be able to go to the desert after all, and that the photographer will be so disappointed because this is her first freelance job and it is falling through, and that the artist will be so disgusted because I have told him I am going to make a book with his painting of the woman and the goats in the desert, and now I'm not even going to come. And I am thinking I am crazy, I am crazy, I have lost my train of thought, I have made myself believe that there is some good to writing stories, too much marijuana has filled my brain with strange ambitions, and on and on until I am gone completely, the apartment is gone, the floor melts, the walls melt, I see the delicate structure like an ice crystal that everything depends on, that the universe rides on, and then the ice melts and I melt and everything is terrible, all sense has completely gone.

But the next morning when I wake up, the sun is out. I get up and have a grapefruit and a cup of coffee. I feel better even though my stomach is messed up and won't digest anything, has been refusing everything before eleven o'clock in the morning, serious symptoms. I will die of nervous ulcers before I am forty-five. Then Leo comes in the door wanting to go to the desert with me after all, tossing around money, even willing to pay for the airplane tickets until my own check comes. But that is the way it is, living with Leo: one day he is a regular-sized man, then the next he becomes big and lionhearted again, capable of large proportions, elastic man.

So that night I settle into a Southwest Airlines economy seat, a cardboard box of files on my lap, Leo tucked in on the wingside with a yellow plastic bag of grapefruit and peanut butter, provisions for the trip, and the plane takes off above all the lights that are Dallas, lurching a little in the air currents, making me think of my own death as airplanes always do, making me think what everyone will say, that I died in my prime, that I still had quite a bit to say, and I wonder if people who die in airplane accidents always have a head full of plans right up to the time of fiery consummation, and then I decide that they do. But then we are very high and the night is black and somewhere above the desert we start slowing, coming down.

The artist's new red car is going to carry us all. He is packing his watercolors, a large pad, sleeping bags for everyone, gloves and a knife so that he can look for peyote at least, he isn't sure there will be anything else. Are you sure she'll be out there, he asks, are there going to be goats? And I always answer yes, that I'm sure, I am getting good at pretending that. The artist is having some problems at the house with his wife. She says Well ex-cuse me! and he says I've had it. He walks out, but Leo and I don't even look up from the packing. Then we pick up the photographer, who just came back from Guatemala, who doesn't have a job at the photo lab anymore and who is shy and doesn't know me very well, and I am amazed again that these people are going with me to a place I have named in the desert to see a woman I have assured them is supposed to heal people with her hands. But then it is the twenty-first century, we're not going for the laying of hands, we're going to lay hands on. If Jesus Christ were living I would write a story about him and sell it to a magazine and get some people out for photographs and sketches, some close-ups of the miracle of laying-on of hands. Leo has divorced himself from the pilgrimage. He is going along for the ride. He has forgotten his camera, his writing tablet and his pen. He will look out of the car windows and count the yuccas while I try to remember what road to take when.

And where are we going? We are tracing out a vague pattern of dirt roads south of Sierra Blanca winding through the Quitman Mountains toward the Rio Grande. I know one dirt road goes to the woman's cabin, which is alone on a ridge looking out over Mayfield Canyon, and another dirt road goes to Indian Hot Springs, down by the river. This is special country, wonderful country, all red rock and huge tumbled stone and mountain cliffs studded with caves first used by river- and rock-loving Indians, now by coyotes and wet-backs. I can remember in one section the river plain spreading out an area of hot springs bubbling out of the ground into twenty-two pools, which Indians declared to be forever neutral ground. At that point in the river, because the springs happen to come up on the northern side of the Rio Grande, there is a rope bridge across the water so that Mexican villagers cross and take baths, too, although the border patrolmen shoot men in the legs for doing that. Even if they are only villagers coming across for the baths, they are nevertheless wet-backs when they cross the river. In that respect a border patrolman is a visionary, taught in geography classes to hold the map of a United States firmly in mind, so that even when he works for a living in a desert that stretches to infinity and upholds a river from both sides, he can still clearly see a sharp black line that cuts it cleanly in half.

But I don't want to go all the way to the river and the hot springs, I want to remember when to make the turn away to the cabin that is the woman's house. Trying to get there, though, I tell the artist to take a turn and then another one and then we get lost. Then another turn, and we're still lost.

Pretty soon we're very lost in the maze of little arroyos criss-crossing paths, which the roads have turned into. In the low parts we all get out, Leo and the photographer and I putting rocks underneath the wheels of the artist's red car so that it will drive over the washed-out places without getting stuck, and we push and the artist revs the engine and gravel comes out, the smell of burning rubber comes up, there is dust, it isn't very funny that we're stuck and lost in the desert. Finally at one arroyo the three of us push so hard the car becomes unstuck again and the artist drives away, drives away in a big cloud of dust, leaving the photographer and Leo and me standing there. The engine fades away over the hill and the desert is quiet, big yuccas bending over us, little scrubby greasewood here and there, lots of sky. So we walk until we get to the top of the hill and he can't be seen. We walk some more and we walk about a mile, then there he is, the red car stopped in the road, the artist sitting down on a rock beside it. He isn't smiling when we walk up. It was sure good to get away from you for a little bit, he says. So we drive on.

The sun is almost down when we finally round a turn, and the tumble of pens and sheds appears on a ridge above us. We make the last climb up the road into a cleared area, a quiet dark cabin in the middle. Nothing is going on. No cars. Some chickens are picking apart a mattress close to the porch door. Half a dozen horses stand bunched together in the mesquite that grows along the edges of the yard, giving us the lookover, and in the back of the cabin somewhere, although I can't see them, I know there are a great number of goats. Leo and the artist and the photographer start wandering around the yard, sniffing around tentatively like humans do trying to get their bearings, trying to locate this and that, peering into the distance at the hills, shuffling through the dirt of the clearing discovering rocks and rusted nails, making mental note of the road where we were before, the large yuccas, the dog with one blue eye and one yellow who flaps his tail around in a circle when I come up to the door and knock. Someone is stirring in the darkness of the porch,

91

but when the door opens it isn't an old woman, it is an old man thin and brown, with white grizzle for a beard, an old blue stocking cap, two black teeth set between two brown ones in the gums. The *señora* he tells me, *no está en la casa.* She was earlier, he says, but she isn't anymore. Well, she will be back sometime, I know that, or maybe she won't be back, but what can we do? We can stay, we can wait, we can look at the goats.

The old man says he herds the goats, which, he waves toward the back, are all in the pens. So I wander back and there they are, hundreds of goats, all different colors and sizes, but more babies than large ones, standing, sitting, bumping each other, watching the photographer and the artist and Leo who are leaning at individual places around the pen. I find my own place and watch them for a long time. They are such beautiful animals, the shades of their coats strange colors, their eyes with the pupils slanted sideways, some blue and some gold, and their mouths smiling, goat buddha smiles. Standing watching them I see that I have come to a place where the four-footed far outnumber the two-footed and where in the large space of sky and canyon even that little differentiation breaks down. So I stand and watch the goats just like they stand and watch me, no more really, though, than they stand and watch each other. Then I watch the photographer and Leo and the artist, all of us watching not saying anything, part of the general herd.

▲

At night the four of us walk into the desert in a loop of goat paths, the moon bright enough so that we can see exactly where we are in relation to the path, the rocks, the hills and the greasewood. The stars swim straightforwardly in a band that sweeps across the night as we walk the eye of the kaleidoscope, enjoying our own black silhouettes jutting out from our feet in the sand. The artist says he has been rolfed and Leo asks what that means. He says it's like zone therapy a little bit, the rolfer finds these places in the body that are sore, then you yell and cry and talk about what you are thinking. The artist says that rolfing is a wonderful thing, that everyone should do rolfing, and Leo believes that the artist has fallen in love with his rolfer, and right after telling about rolfing, he mentions love, that we're taught not to do it. The photographer agrees, but she doesn't say too much because she doesn't talk as much as everyone else, although she says yes, yes, intently at times and nods her head. Leo is agreeing too, that's true, we haven't been taught to love, and I say yes, that's true, because everyone's afraid that if it's okay to love everybody then we'll all wind up going to bed with our fathers and mothers as well as our neighbor's wife. Everyone agrees, so we are quiet and think about that for a while, walking along the path of illuminated rocks, crunching along, someone picking up something, rubbing it in the palm. Look, the artist says, let's sit down together and make a circle, so we sit down in a circle in the path but it is silly. We hold hands but Leo yawns, I hunker down, feel like the stars are breathing down my neck, crunch rocks, cough a little. Finally the artist says maybe we should get up. Leo says, It's just that I've got a little stiffness in my back. Walking is better, the artist says, the photographer agrees.

Then the clearing edge again, the four of us stepping into its circle, three of the horses stepping into it from the other side, looking at us, us looking at them. Two gangs. They are spread out in a semicircle, the middle one white—white in the moonlight like an apparition, like the horse of a thousand stories, charmed, made from wind or the foam of an ocean that the desert used to sit at the bottom of. It seems to me that they are saying something to us, or maybe waiting for us to say something, and I look at the white one, in the middle of its head, but there is no more than a general concentration between his head and mine, lowered at each other. Then he bows and turns into the desert. The two brown ones leave, as well, and we go into the cabin where the goatherder is already preparing for bed. He shows the photographer that she can have the couch where he himself sleeps.

The couch is against the wall of the kitchen, piled with a brown scrap of blanket in the darkest corner, lit only by the kerosene flame in the lamp the goatherder holds while he shows her. But she declines, it is too dark, the folds of the rags too mysterious. She shares the mattress on the porch with Leo and me, the artist sleeping at the side of the bed in a sleeping bag, sounds of shifting animals outside the screen, the goatherder's horse taking a long piss right by the door, finally the photographer snoring, the artist breathing loudly, Leo's breath on my neck.

The morning comes before the sun. It is grey and rose, the black and white rooster is crowing from a yucca near the porch. He has a bright brown neck and red wattles. When I walk out in the yard, there are little chickens, a solitary duck, an eccentric of his own kind taken to the desert, and two guinea hens. Also cows, silly and brown, wandering across the lot. There is the smell of coffee, which the goatherder is making in a charred pot, there are the goats in the pen, butting and baaing, rustling and kneeling and gazing, the babies by their mothers, the young males leaping and kicking, everyone waiting for the goatherder to come and open up the gate so they can go. Then the sun is up, the goatherder saddles his own horse, his stocking cap slung to the back of his head like a blue flag, and lets out the goats. They are tumbling through the clearing, beating up the dust. Leo is suddenly running down into the desert with them, zig-zagging through the mesquite and over the rocks, a goat himself with his own long legs leaping and flapping. But the cows can't go, the goatherder beats them away from the path the goats took down the arroyo with a stick. The rest of the day they peer out over the mesas, not knowing quite what to do with themselves because they aren't goats and aren't allowed to go with the herd. Then the clearing quiets again and the goatherder is gone on his horse. Leo comes walking back up the path, the rest of us looking out over the hills to the last of the goats disappearing around a bend, and the sun is all the way up. There is no old woman here, but there is the desert, there is sun, there were goats until just a few minutes ago, their dust and smell and images still in the air.

And in the afternoon the woman comes. Before she came, I was worrying, I was thinking this isn't really a wise old woman, this is a silly old woman I am waiting for, sometimes she repeats herself and sometimes she makes wrong decisions, and really I have never seen her heal anybody, I have seen her touch them, but I haven't seen anything. But on the other hand, does that matter anyway? The photographer asks me if this woman really heals people and I tell her that I don't know. For photographs it doesn't matter anyway. But then the old woman comes driving up in a dusty station wagon, and a small man runs around from the driver's seat when the car stops to open her door. Her body is still solid and good. She has a heavy scarf on her head, I remember now that she always wears it over her hair like that, her eyes are blue and she is smiling and happy to see me although we are suddenly shy when we hug each other. I tell her this is the artist and this is the photographer. She hugs Leo because she knows him. So that afternoon the photographer tells her to stand there and stand there, and she stands. Then the photographer tells her to stand by the goats, which have come back, and she stands by them. She picks the little ones up, and the photographer takes photographs of that, and puts them down, and the photographer gets that, too. Then the photographer tells her to heal a person, and the artist sits on the chair. The woman puts her hands on his head and on his back, she sits and looks at him a little, then she moves her hands on his shoulders. The artist says that something flies out of his right eye. She tells him that something left, and he says does it really happen that way, does it really fly out? She says sometimes it does, flying out of an eye or the mouth. Then Leo says, you should tell her about your stomach. I say yes, well, I've been having a nervous stomach, I can't eat in the morning. So she tells me to sit in a chair. She sits in a chair near the screen, the rooster looking over her shoulder, Leo getting some coffee. And suddenly I am farting, I am belching, the juices in my stomach are rolling and roaring, I am getting louder by the second, belching and farting and growling. I put my head down in my hands because it is very embarrassing. The photographer laughs, Leo comes out of the kitchen to see what is going on. The woman looks at me, smiling. She says do you want me to take that away now? I say of course. She tells me to lie down on the mattress on my back, she passes her hands over me from my head to my toes, then shakes her fingers at the foot of the bed, shaking all the noise away, everything finally quieting down, my stomach stopped.

Finally there is no more film and the woman sits in her chair on the porch, eighty years old telling about the goats, what they've been doing. Her friend drove her out to the camp. He's a barber and fiddler from Sierra Blanca, out in the yard talking to the goatherder. He tells me he's going to leave and be with his children in Del Rio, she says, but maybe he won't. I get out the bottle of champagne and everyone drinks some, the goatherder comes in, a little for everyone. This is the first champagne the woman has ever had, the first alcoholic beverage in eighty years of life, my responsibility. I'm tampering here with history, major heroine legend in the making. *Anglo curandera* and desert wise woman, turns to booze at the age of eighty years, toxifies her system irreparably, transforming her delicately balanced system of healing to a jumble of pickled nerves. But she takes some sips, gets happy. We're going to make some money on this book, she says.

Maybe you'll stay here, I tell her friend, maybe you won't want to be taken care of by your family after all.

May-*be*, he says, always may-be so.

▲

Sometimes I think about Dallas while I'm sitting in the back seat of the artist's red car, looking out the window at the Rio Grande, driving along. I wonder if Shorty will have stopped outside the apartment door, sniffed the marijuana and busted Morgani, thrown him out, barred the door. Probably not, but may-be so. The road is gravel, adobes of Mexican villages and single desert farmers along the other side, rocky cliffs on our side, red canyons, dry creekbeds running to the river in a tumble of rocks, the air blue, the salt cedar feathering green for spring along the river, the desert red and brown. Then I think about the Rio Grande itself, how it is just a trickle of water, barely visible through the screen of salt cedar that stretches out between the riverbed and the road. I have read that when the Spanish missionaries first came to this valley, the river was so wide they could barely see the other side, and the grass was tall as a man's head. I think that some day someone should dynamite all the dams on the upper Rio Grande and let the water come down as it should, flooding half of Las Cruces, all of El Paso downtown, a terrible large roll of water that would eventually settle itself into a wide-running band, to make all of this desert green again. And I am looking out over the river when a bird comes down. I see him suspended in the air, his wings spread out, only moving them every few seconds once or twice to maintain his spot above the riverbed.

We all see it, the artist sees it, he slows down, I grab his shoulder, the photographer says Wow and Look at that and Leo cranes his head around. We're all looking at that bird, the sun on such a beam above us that it illuminates his wings to translucent red and brown, his head completely white, so that I realize it has to be an eagle. It's an eagle, I say, it's really an eagle, I can't believe it is an eagle. Maybe it's a hawk of some kind Leo says. No it's not, it's an eagle, I tell him. I'm looking at it, everyone's looking at it, and the eagle is looking at us, he is suspended in the air and he has a direct eye on what must appear to him as a wonderful shiny red object full of chattering animals that has stopped in the middle of the road. The artist lets the car roll a little closer, and the bird moves in a little closer. Then when he stops, we do, too. High above him another one just like him appears, circling at the same distance but on a higher plane.

Then we know something at the same time—we need to get out quick. The artist is already out, and Leo is out on the other side, the photographer and I are scrambling out, then we're in the middle of the road in a little group, all looking at the incredible illuminated bird. So as the bird stands still in the air, the sun beaming like a sword through his heart pinning him against the blue field. I get an old ecstatic feeling of being overcome, like when holy fire comes down in a church service and the people cry out, tears in their eyes, falling down on the ground, until I can hardly see the bird anymore. But I realize what is happening and I think no tears, no tears, I want to see him as clearly as I possibly can. Then just in that instant we are face to face, on the same plane somewhere very high, and I am eyeing the eagle, the Aztec bird coasting over the two-headed stream of red and blue that is the stream of the desert and the stream of the river, one embracing the other and the sky embracing everything. The bird swoops down almost into the water he has been hanging over, angles in front of us, crosses the road, swoops behind a hill, back up, above us, suddenly down, around us, above us again, and away. Then he is gone. We are standing, looking up at the sky still for a space of time, in the middle of the road.

▲▲▲▲▲▲

DESCENT
INTO
BROTHERLAND

Oh, South Dallas VA Hospital, red brick buildings blocks long and blocks wide with many wings, where the war-broken men wheel up and down the high-waxed grey-tiled corridors, without legs, without arms, without eyes sometimes, hundreds of would-have-been-beautiful-well-made men come to the hospital from that place called War: off-limits to women except those whose homes have been chosen in some male poker game parlor Pentagon as a good War Zone. So the women who came to the VA hospital are rarely there on their own account, but come instead with their husbands and lovers and brothers, the men leaning against the women with canes, holding the women's hands, the women wheeling the chairs, the women writing out papers for them, just like me coming with my brother Okie because his appointment slips come stamped in red TO BE ACCOMPANIED BY A FAMILY MEMBER, the two of us in the van he drove down from Oklahoma pulling into the parking lot.

Now I've visited Okie in the brig before, I've visited Okie in the psychiatric wards, and I've visited Okie in the Oklahoma jail, and I've talked to the lawyers and jail wardens and policemen and psychiatric boards and judges. So I'm only a little bit nervous about talking to this VA psychiatrist about Okie's VA check, which hasn't been coming for the right amount of disability since he got out of jail.

Okie kills the engine. I stare out the passenger side window at this mausoleum/museum for the relics of war, the junkyard of the war machine, six stories of hospital walls, drink down the last of my Winchell's Donuts coffee like a final fortification, a little caffeine vigor for my knock at the hospital door. Oh excuse me Mr. Doctor, Mr. Bandaids-For-The-Millions-While-Top-Brass-Plan-The-Bombs-And-Clean-Their-Fingernails, I hate to bring it up, but my brother here still has something coming from when he worked for you and I've come to help him collect what's still due.

Okie is already out the door. He is standing by the van pulling his Harley shirt over his head. He wads it up, throws it into the back of the van on the mattress where he's been sleeping since he got out of jail five months ago. He shuffles through the tools cardboard junk food beer can slush behind my seat, pulls out a faded yellow pullover, dirty with oil but doesn't say Harley.

The doctor might give me a hard time if I don't change, he says. Doctors, he says while we're walking up the front walk, think you're weird if you ride a motorcycle. They see all kinds of things in it. They think you have a death wish.

Like women and horses, I say for the sake of saying, doctors think women who like horses go for big studs.

100

I don't see why they don't think the same thing about cars, he says. More people are killed in cars than they are on motorcycles.

Doctors like to see symbols, I say like I'm the one to explain all social phenomena to him in generalizations. We are walking in the lobby where men are lounging in robes smoking cigarettes, talking with children who aren't allowed upstairs. There is a maze of corridors, signs and arrows to labs and offices, waiting rooms, blood units, x-ray wards, pharmacies, long lines of men in front of windows, rooms full of men waiting to hear certain numbers called. We find room one fourteen, the magic entry number of Okie's appointment slip, where a nurse tells us to wait in the hall. Men are lined up on both sides leaning against the walls, so we find a little space and join them. A blond long-hair is on Okie's other side, offers him a match for a cigarette. I don't listen to what he is saying until I hear Okie tell him something about Thorazine. Then I hear them say some other drug names, and Okie names some symptoms: dry mouth, dizziness, can't read, can't think, can't stand up. The long-hair agrees. So I understand that he's come to get a change in his prescription and is shopping around for a better drug.

The doors at the end of the corridor swing open and three men appear, two with nurse smocks on either side of a small black-haired man, nervous pretty Rosita-kind-of-woman trailing behind. They are almost to where we are standing, the black-haired man no more than two feet away from me, the nurse-man on my side even closer, and I am looking in the black-haired man's face like everyone does in this hospital, wondering what his problem is when there are no arms or legs or other parts of the body missing. He looks straight ahead like he doesn't see anyone, when his eyes widen just a little bit, as if a realization of where he is has just struck him, and his body falls back like he has just been hit with a two-by-four, jerking out of the nurse-men's arms, the back of his head thudding against the floor, his legs rigid, locked at the knees. His Rosita-woman goes down on her knees to help him, but the nurse-men push her out of the way. Then the man's legs begin kicking out, trying to kick the legs of the nurse-men away from him, his arms flailing. I can't see his face for the nurse-men's backs who are leaning over him, their own elbows pushing around. Another nurse-man appears, all three of them leaning over the man I can't see, except for his legs and feet, which are pushing up and down along the gray floor tiles trying to push themselves backward, back up the corridor the way they came in. A few long seconds of flailing and pushing and grunting, me flat against the wall watching the feet kicking in black polished shoes so close to my own. Then the nurse-men come up again with him in the middle, his mouth closed, his face as calm and impenetrable as when he first came in. They walk past me and Okie, each nurse-man now with two arms around each of the black-haired man's, and they're about three paces past when his body goes stiff and lunges again, his head flung back so hard that I can see his entire face upside down, his legs pedaling against the floor. The nurse-men don't lose their grip this time though. They follow him down, roll him onto his chest, pin one of his arms back, hold his head down. A security guard appears and then another, and equipment comes—a straitjacket and a wheelchair—and pretty soon the black-haired man is sitting in the wheelchair wearing the strait-jacket and the last few feet of the corridor are traveled. He is wheeled through the set of doors at the end surrounded by guards, the Rosita-woman crying, walking by herself two or three steps behind them, no one paying any attention to her, no one saying anything to her during the whole little drama, until she gets to the set of doors herself when one of the security guards turns to her and tells her to wait in the hall.

The men along the walls shift. Someone laughs a little, and I am thinking why was he so scared, there aren't any operating rooms in there or labs, there are only office spaces for the doctors. And I say to Okie, well, that guy sure didn't want to see the doctor, trying to get Okie to tell me what it was that the black-haired man must have suddenly thought about. But Okie says oh, he was just a troublemaker, no tolerance in his voice for the man who hasn't learned yet what Okie has learned, that trouble makes for trouble and the man who kicks in the VA hospital gets his head kicked in.

So we lean against the wall, Okie smokes cigarettes, I go out and bring coffee in, I buy a newspaper and read it, Okie buys a Hershey, goes to the bathroom, I go to the bathroom, I pick up the newspaper again and read the classifieds. Finally when time has become meaningless Okie's number is called and we go into a room where Dr. Mengle is waiting.

Are you his sister? Dr. Mengle asks. Dr. Mengle is not a man; she is a woman about my age with frizzed-up hair like mine, who doesn't know war anymore than I do except from what we read in books and get from the brother/news. I say Yes and smile and sit down. Okie starts looking at the floor and swinging his head. When he looks at her, he looks at her sideways, and when she asks him questions, he waits too long to say anything.

Is he always like this? She makes a little face at me.

I wait too long to answer, too, and she goes back to him, ticking off the questions fast, as though she has already asked them lots of times today.

Have you ever heard voices no one else around you was hearing? He shakes his head. I wonder about the devil in Los Angeles, why Okie isn't telling her about the devil talk the way he once told me and the way I know he has told other psychiatrists, because it is in the copy of his file our father keeps and has shown me. And I think maybe Okie should tell her about that one, or I should remind him. But then when the devil came maybe there was no one else in the room to hear or not to hear, so maybe that's why Okie doesn't think it is the answer to what she is asking. Before I can really figure it out, Dr. Mengle goes on to the next question.

Have you ever felt that someone was controlling your thoughts?

I *know*, Okie says after waiting for a while, studying his shoes, that someone is.

How do they do it?

No reply.

Do they do it to everybody or just to you?

Everybody. Well. He thinks it over. Everybody but mostly me.

Is it a person who is in control?

Okie is frowning. He concentrates on the floor between his boots. She is looking at the same file our father has. I am following the scenario. The file says Okie has been told to do certain things by a voice from the moon, and I am sure Dr. Mengle has read this and wants to hear him say it all over again. But I can see he isn't going to say that this time, he is shaking his head and looking distracted, staring at the floor.

Dr. Mengle has run out of time on that question anyway.

Are you receiving any medication?

I was, but I'm not taking it.

She puts down her file and taps her pencil on the desk. And why not? Don't you want to get well?

I heard on the television it wasn't any good.

Who told you that?

People.

What did they say?

They said that medicine like I was taking will fuck you up.

They're lying then, Mr. Lester. What were you taking?
Thorazine.

Thorazine is a wonderful drug for mood control.
Valium.

Valium is the best antidepressant we have. She tosses her head a little. Unless the patients abuse it. She squints at Okie. So why did you want to come in today?

He doesn't say anything. I clear my throat. He wants to see about his VA check. He hasn't been getting it at one hundred percent evaluation. A paper came that said he wasn't evaluated at one hundred percent anymore, and there hadn't been any physical reevaluation. So we wrote and got a slip back saying he should come in to be examined.

Oh well, she says. I can see he's a hundred percent. She taps the file. Everyone here has rated him a hundred percent. I'll certainly say a hundred percent. She has a pad of notepaper with the name of a drug across the top: HALODOL in large blue letters. She writes an address on it and hands it to me. Just write the adjudication officer about that. He'll find out what's wrong.

So, Mr. Lester. She leans back in her chair. Is there any special problem that's bothering you right now?

Okie's shoulders bunch up and he looks up at me. I suddenly feel heavy, woozy with weight. I nod my head a little. I think you should tell her, I say without any sound. He looks over at her for the first time. She is looking down at her clipboard.

Have you gotten anything from Oklahoma City? he asks.

She starts leafing through the file, shaking her head. No. Waco, Waco, San Diego, Dallas, no nothing here.

I finally say I think he's wondering about an incident that happened in Oklahoma that the VA psychiatrists up there asked him about.

Okie leans toward me, hanging on the edge of his chair like he is trying to get me to say what he can't, and his need is so hot and close to the surface that it is burning everything in my mind away, my suspicions and fear and anger at the VA hospital, at the navy, at the world the way it is gone for an instant, and I am only thinking here is a *doctor*, Okie, like the word itself will make him well, a *doctor*, a *doctor*, a *doctor*, tell her that the Thorazine and Valium and hospital visits aren't working, tell her that you killed a man, and it wasn't in Vietnam, either, it was in Oklahoma, and it happened just five months ago.

Okie's mouth hangs open like he needs more air.

Well, don't worry, she says, flipping the file shut because that was that. The last question. If you were admitted to the hospital in Oklahoma we'll be getting the papers soon. It always takes a little while.

She stands up, signaling it is time for us to stand up, too.

I'm recommending you come in, Mr. Lester. It

105

shouldn't take more than a couple of days. I'm not one for keeping a man in the hospital any more than he needs to be. But we need to match the drugs you are taking to your individual biology. On an outpatient basis that could take months. In a hospital only a couple of days. She is walking us to the door. Thank you for coming, Mrs. Taylor. You tell him he needs to come in.

My face is burning. She is showing us out. Okie is in front of me, already through the door. I try to tell her all right, I'll tell him, but I am choking. I can't talk. My fist, I am thinking, should go through this door. I nod at her and then I am in the hallway, walking down the hall on the high-polished linoleum tile. Wait, wait, I am thinking and I stop. I've got to stop it. I need to go back and shake her. I need to shake her very hard and tell her something, tell her to listen! Tell her she's just not listening! Okie is walking down the hall. I am stopped. Her door is still open. He is going to the lab. He looks back and waves me to come on. We walk on down the hall and I sit down on a chair, the fact that we got what we came for—one hundred percent—completely forgotten, while Okie swims in the sea of disabled men and disappears by himself through a door.

A
CALL
FROM
BROTHERLAND

This is the way I think it started: word got around certain parts of Oklahoma City that on the first of every month Okie received eight hundred dollars and ninety tabs of Valium from the U.S. government for a craziness that Veterans Administration psychiatrists attributed to the Vietnam War. Now even without the money and the drugs, Okie would have had friends. Lovern Evetts was his friend; they had played in the high school band together before Okie dropped out and joined the navy. Lovern had a certain understanding of Okie and a certain love. He had gone to Vietnam himself and had been given a Medal of Honor, which he buried in his parents' storage room and refused to wear, even for the families of old friends when he shouldered their boxed-up sons in military funerals. But Vietnam hadn't made him crazy, at least not certifiably so, or at least whatever wounds his brain had received had been nursed and nurtured by his own family, who owned a block in an Oklahoma City suburb where the father ran a used-car lot and the mother ran a barbeque pit and Lovern was eventually given a mechanic shop to run. Okie's family lived in different towns and communicated with one another only in sparse and erratic bursts of holiday transcendence and then with great difficulty, which is why Okie didn't really think too much about looking any of them up when he walked off the gangplank in San Diego. Instead he went to the only family who would really give him a sailor's welcome, the California motorcycle black-leather brotherhood of veterans and dropouts nobody else took care of, so they learned to take care of one another as best they could by manufacturing experiences so intense as to distract themselves from the sorrow of recollection. He stayed with them until the Vietnam wounds of his brain were completely fried, cauterized with alcohol and acid, visions of chain beatings, blood in the alleys, hot steel, friends dead of heroin overdoses in muggy L.A. tenement-motels overlaying the old Vietnam wounds with hot red layers of new skin.

One day Okie saw a biker brother shot down by a jealous woman on the front steps of a house nobody knew who paid the rent on die slowly while begging someone to open the door, which nobody did. Okie finally opened it when the man became still, and dragged him into the living room. Then Okie and two other men left out the back door before the cops came. Shortly after that, Okie began to see the devil, the devil licking at the wound in his brain that had never healed right, making hell itself spew out in visions of friends left to maggots in the shag carpets of living rooms like piles of half-eaten junk food and women with blow torches for hands. So he turned himself in to a navy psychiatric ward, asking for electroshock treatments to block out whatever was left of his brain. But they gave him over to the Veterans Administration, who prescribed money and drugs instead and put him out on the streets again. At least he didn't go back to California. Instead he went to Oklahoma, where he looked up his old friend Lovern. Lovern's father, a veteran himself from a different war, let Okie sleep at the used-car lot at night as a security guard. Lovern's mother gave him barbeque ribs to eat. Lovern himself let Okie keep his Harley in back of the mechanic shop and let him do freelance welding on the motorcycles that came in. If Okie had never found any friends other than Lovern and Lovern's mother and father, he still would have been more fortunate than other Vietnam veterans, many who haven't to this day found a good friend.

But of course lots of friends started hanging around Okie once they discovered how generous he was with a Veterans Administration check based on one hundred percent disability. Maybe they thought his brain was a little slow, maybe he didn't change his clothes often, maybe he didn't wash his hair very much or trim his beard. But he had a good-looking black Harley Davidson, which impressed the Oklahoma bikers, and he liked to spread his money around, which impressed the biker women, and he didn't like to take three Valiums a day, as Dr. Outlaw at the outpatient's clinic had recommended, so he gave most of them away, which impressed everyone who liked pills. So Okie's circle of friends began to grow, and more and more bikers began showing up at Lovern's mechanic shop to hang out.

Lovern's father didn't like this much. He said this crowd of people would only get Lovern and Okie into trouble. And Lovern's mother didn't like it. She told one man she wouldn't give him barbeque so long as he wore a swastika on his belt buckle. We fought a war to get rid of that, she said. But Lovern liked the bikers. They liked to smoke joints and drink beer, and to roar around the Oklahoma countryside on the weekends and build bonfires and have parties in country houses. Lovern even bought a motorcycle himself and a black leather riding outfit, and a black leather jacket and cap for his five-year-old boy to wear on Sunday drives. Then one day a man appeared who even Lovern recognized as trouble, the friend of a friend of Okie's, just in town from California. His name was Thieving John, and he made a living selling motor-cycle parts to the same biker friends it was rumored he stole them from, although no one could really catch him. This was just after the first of the month, and Okie put his Valiums in the drawer of Lovern's desk, and on a day John had been hanging around they turned up missing. Okie might have said something to John and John said something back. Someone shoved and someone punched and suddenly both men were down on the floor. Okie had a tire arm in his hand, which Lovern grabbed from above him and took away. Everyone knew then that Okie and Thieving John didn't get along well.

Neither Okie nor Thieving John really wanted to see each other. Thieving John stopped coming around Lovern's mechanic shop, to the relief of everyone and most especially Lovern's father and mother, and Okie took to checking if Thieving John was going to be at someone's house or party before he came to visit, since the biker family in Oklahoma City was relatively small, so that everyone knew everyone else. But there is a kind of personality that enjoys creating the circumstances for trouble, and unfortunately such a woman was a part of this circle of biker friends that had grown around Okie and Lovern. She decided she would throw a big party for everyone and roast a baby goat in her backyard. So she called up the shop and invited Okie to the party. Okie asked her if Thieving John was going to be there, and she said no. Then when Okie agreed to come, she called up John and invited him.

Who knows what she was looking for—maybe just a few hot words or a roll-around-on-the-floor kind of fight, maybe she was thinking after all both are my friends, aren't they, so I have to invite them both, or maybe she wasn't really thinking about it, just letting her mind ride high and blank in opened-out anticipation. So when Okie walked in the front door, the first man he saw was John. He went back out and got a revolver from a bag on his motorcycle and brought it back in the house. But the woman who was looking for trouble who was barbequing the goat told Okie there couldn't be guns around because there were little children present. She took the gun from Okie and put it on the mantel shelf. That's the way the party began.

There was too much booze, of course, too much barbeque, too much talking, too many people milling around, and sometime in the early morning John and Okie found themselves together in the garage. Lovern and his wife and five-year-old son had already gone home about an hour before, and there were only four or five people left at the party, a couple of them passed out. There was one other man out in the garage, and he heard Okie say something to John, and then John pointed at Okie's Harley. See that bike? the man remembered John saying. It's going to be mine someday soon, and it'll be painted red as your own blood. So there was some pushing and a scuffle and some more words. John broke away and went into the kitchen. Okie went out the garage door, came into the house again through the front door, and took his pistol off the mantel shelf. He walked into the kitchen, put the pistol to the back of John's head and pulled the trigger. Two men at the table were talking to John when it happened, and the woman who wanted to see trouble was sitting in a rocker by the kitchen door with her three-year-old girl in her lap and looked into the kitchen just in time to see the back of Thieving John's head become a red bloom. Okie put the gun in his belt and walked out the door, apparently stunned by the weight of his own action, called murder in the first degree with four witnesses, which, in Oklahoma, can bring a penalty of death in the electric chair.

About three hundred miles south from this house where the party was held, was a white clapboard house on the edge of town, a peach orchard on one side of it and a garden on the other. There were tearoses growing across the back bedroom window. And there was a rooster crowing about seven o'clock in the morning, when I woke from a dream of walking up and down streets in a grey foggy dawn in a city unfamiliar to me looking for my brother, thinking something was wrong. Finally I found him sitting in a car that wasn't his parked at a curb. He was staring out the window like he was in shock, his body slack, as though he couldn't have moved it even if he had wanted to. So I wasn't a body myself, more like a spirit, easily slipping through car walls, clamoring around him looking at his face and his glazed-out eyes asking over and over what was wrong. But he kept on staring out the window until the alarm went off and I woke up. Chuck was still asleep on his back holding my hand. But I shook him awake and began to tell him what I had been dreaming. A ringing came from the kitchen, and when I got out of bed and answered, Lovern Evetts calling from Oklahoma, his voice overfull with emotion, to tell me how my brother Okie shot a man last night and walked out of the house, police dragneting the woods for him, and nobody knew where he had gone.

▲▲▲▲▲▲

KINGDOM COME

Shorty and Evelyn are a true landlord couple. She sits at the front office desk all day balancing books, watching a tiny TV and answering the telephone, while Shorty loads ladders and tools on and off his pickup truck, taking off from the front curb of the apartment house sidewalk and coming back, then a few hours later taking off again in a restless patrol of his web of twenty-eight apartment houses clustered in the neighboring blocks. When I go down to pay my rent, Evelyn is always in the office, and Shorty is either coming in or going out. Once I go down in the evening to slip the check under the door, but Evelyn is still up, sitting in a loose kimono with a cloth around her head, squinting in the low light.

I always leave this shade down, she says, when I'm in here at night. I was down here once when I looked up and there in the door were two terrible-looking things, they were Mexicans just looking in here. Get on out of here, I said, we're closed, and one of them says, but don't you have any rooms to rent? And I said to him Don't you see that sign? We're closed. So finally he went. But girl, I tell you, I was scared. So that's why I just keep this blind closed here all the time.

If I should see Evelyn in the hall, she is always ready with a fast tirade on one of her favorite subjects—the various ways she finds dark-skinned human beings objectionable, or the various feats Shorty has done within the structure of the Hard-Sell Baptist Church. I hear the story of Shorty's time in prison and how bad his drinking and brawling were several times, how the Baptist Church saved him and made him a deacon, how God's grace gave him the twenty-eight apartment houses he has today. I get to see photographs of a certificate changing hands between Shorty and a man in a minister's suit. I get to hear how apartment renters torment Shorty all the time, calling him in the middle of the night to fix things. And I even get a report on how trashed out Apartment F is upstairs where that blond-haired man with the motorcycle moved in, she had to go into the place for something and it was a mess! And I say well, I think most men don't keep their apartments clean, especially when they first leave home. Naw, that's not true, she says. You should see Julian's in Apartment A, he keeps his apartment perfect. And of course she's right. Julian lounges in white tennis shorts on his window ledge in the evenings, half-open windows showing purple velvet curtains, gilt mirrors, white walls.

So I try not to see her because of her fast stories, and Shorty because of the list of apartment rules he carries in his pocket. Also because with money coming into our hands, with Leo and Morgani and me all working hard, good Colombian marijuana is also coming in. We smoke it in the walk-in closet so the smoke won't go out the living room door vent into the hall, but the smell of marijuana is everywhere. I can smell it in my clothes now, whiffs of it while I'm walking around because the smoke has permeated the closet, my hair, it is in everything. The walls of the apartment are so thin that I can hear Ira across the hall saying Praise the Lord! and Please God! when he is talking on his telephone, as no doubt he hears us talking sin, which I know he passes on to Evelyn. So I take to leaving through the back door, never walking down the front hallways if I hear a door close or footsteps on the stairs.

Still, Shorty catches me sometimes. Once he follows me down into the basement while I am doing my laundry. He says Ira tells him there are too many men coming in and out of my apartment, there is something wrong with me. And Shorty says, I told him that she was all right, there wasn't anything going on in there. And then somehow the conversation turns to girls, and Shorty tells me that a couple of girls in the apartment have propositioned him, but he didn't have the heart to throw them out.

After all, young girls get lonely, I say.

Sure, he shrugs his shoulders, smiles.

There's been lots of times, he says, these young girls have just seen me like a father. They'll come down to the apartment on Saturday morning, well, maybe not recently, but they used to. They'd have coffee and talk.

He says that sometime I should come down for coffee, and I promise I will. He stands still, his hands on the top of the washing machine smiling at me with a gap-toothed smile, short and mean but not completely unattractive, easy enough to see how young girls might mistake the wide grin lines of his mouth forged in the heat of anger and lust as a smile of welcome and desire forged instead from the heat of love. But I can tell the difference, all right, and I gave him back a good bar-toothed smile of my own, holding the laundry basket to me like a breast plate, up the stairs and slipping away. But he is everywhere, always watching me coming and going. I can see him looking out his upstairs window at me when I go to work in the morning. He stops friends in the hall, asks them why they're in the building. I hear him shuffling up and down outside my door. So every night Morgani and I blow smoke in the closet to the gods of marijuana, asking for enough vegetable strength to keep us mellow, to be nice to Shorty and Evelyn, so that they don't come into our apartment with a passkey looking for our marijuana, and clear from what follows condemn us straight to prison or hell with a formal escort of demons suited out as Dallas cops.

Shorty has also begun to stew about Morgani. After all, the rules clearly state no more than two people to an efficiency apartment, there's three in ours, and Morgani was supposed to leave when he got a job. In fact, Morgani did get a job at a car wash, but why should he move out when he and Leo and I are making the rent payments pretty well together, it is a symbiotic familial relationship, we are making it, dependent on each other, yet on our own. So I tell Morgani, now just don't tell Shorty you've got a job.

But Shorty bugs Morgani every time he sees him in the hall with this routine, have you got a job yet boy, have you got a job. Finally I go down to Shorty's apartment. Evelyn answers the door. I have it all figured out in advance since Shorty's basement conversation, so I have my coffee cup in my hand, big smile, can I come in for a Saturday cup if I bring my own?

Evelyn smiles and lets me in. Two blond-haired girls are sprawled out asleep on the couch. She puts her finger to her mouth and leads me to the dining table on the opposite side of the room. Those are my granddaughters, she says, they sleep here on the weekends. Of course they can't stay any more than that because it's against the apartment rules.

There are also two yellow and green canaries in a cage by the window. I wave to them genially. Hello little birds. Shorty comes out of the kitchen. I say well, Morgani tells me you were a little angry because he was living here—

Oh no, I'm not angry, he says, it's just that you said he was getting a job, then maybe he would get his own apartment.

Shorty has lots of rooms he could rent, the wife says, there's a good house just a few blocks away, all good Christian men . . .

The problem, I say, is that Morgani is going blind—maybe you two didn't know that.

Oh no, Evelyn says, I didn't know that.

Shorty shakes his head. Well, now see there, I didn't know that either.

Have you ever noticed his eyes?

Oh, I never look at those kinds of things, she says.

Well, it is something we're all adjusting to, I tell them, we are going to the Center for the Blind.

Oh we have a very good friend who is with the Lighthouse . . .

Well, I tell her, this is just like the Lighthouse, but it's the Center. They're going to put Morgani in an apprentice program and do things with him, but it's all going to take some time.

Well, don't you worry about it, Shorty says, now that we understand what's going on it's all right, it's just that rules are rules, but we can make exceptions. And Evelyn nods herself, but she is a little stunned, as though she has never heard Shorty say this before, like the laws of the universe have been suddenly changed and she has just felt the first faint shift in gravity's weight in the seat of her ample behind.

But she rallies and grabs a photograph album I haven't seen before, with photographs of Shorty standing with men holding fiddles at a South Texas fiddler contest, of Shorty standing in a suit with the two blond girls I saw asleep on the couch dressed in white dresses and holding Easter baskets, and of Shorty and Evelyn with hats on and Sunday clothes standing in front of the apartment house. I tell them the photographs are wonderful, and I talk some more to their birds. I even go over to the birdcage and tap on the door.

117

They are very pretty, such cute little round eyes and quick necks. Evelyn says, you have got to go with us to church, just once, to see how you would like it. And I say Oh maybe sometime. Shorty says how about this Sunday, and I say no, I just don't feel like it right now, and Evelyn says, well, maybe later. So finally my coffee is all drunk up. They want to make me some more, but I say no. When I get back to the apartment, I tell Morgani not to worry, I told Shorty and Evelyn that he was going blind.

Later when Shorty sees Morgani standing out waiting for his ride to the car wash where he works, Shorty asks about the apprentice program at the Center for the Blind, and Morgani says, oh it's really great, they're teaching me computer science by hooking me up to a machine and letting me hear all the programming instead of reading it out.

Shorty says uh-hunh! And doesn't ask him anymore.

But then Morgani starts talking about buying a car. I say Morgani, you can't drive a car because Shorty would see you. And Morgani says, he's seen me drive a car before.

He has?

Morgani nods his head. I drove my car wash supervisor's car home two days ago, and Shorty was outside watering.

Right now Morgani doesn't have enough money for a car, and maybe our lease will be up before he does. I advise him to spend the money on his guitar, but this causes me to continue stewing, the pressure of landlord deception weighing heavy, this state of existence, I think to myself, over and over, cannot last.

Leo doesn't smoke marijuana, he smokes cigars. Marijuana, he says, gives him asthma. So he leaves the apartment and goes down to read and write in his journal at Winchell's Donuts to clear out his sinuses with short snorts of exhaust fumes on the walk down Gaston Avenue. He mentions that every time he goes to Winchell's Donuts these days he sees Shorty there drinking coffee, talking to the Chicana behind the counter, who is very pretty, with her curly hair. Once when Leo and I come into Winchell's together, Shorty's hand is on top of hers by the drip coffeepot on the counter. When he sees us, he pulls his hand away. How you doing, Leo? he says, and Leo says he's doing just fine.

After we pay for our coffee and two plain to go, Shorty follows us out onto the parking lot. You ever seen the inside of that one? He points to an apartment building across from Winchell's called the Gaston Arms. I say no, and he says well, come on in and I'll show you around. He walks into a little room on the ground floor with a separate entrance. It has a neat little bed in the middle of one wall made up with a quilt, a refrigerator, a scarf on the chest of drawers. I stay here sometimes, he says, squirming around and smiling at Leo and me, with my girl when she's finished working the counter.

So you have twenty-eight apartments and twenty-eight rooms, I say.

Oh Pat, he says, now you'll really get me in trouble.

Like having a mansion, I say, except that it's spread out.

We walk back past Winchell's and through the front window I can see the curly black-haired girl working behind the counter. She is pouring coffee for a customer, and she looks very young, maybe seventeen, but she's learned how to get her rent paid. Back at the apartment I prance into the doorway, and then I prance around the room, calling Morgani, pacing and posing and waving my arms and saying *well* . . . several times in the course of the story, finally telling him I don't think we have to worry about smoking marijuana anymore, because Shorty has more or less told us that he is a rule breaker, too.

One day a short time after that, Shorty's pickup truck is gone, and Evelyn has closed the office while she is locked up in her apartment. Julian from Apartment A is lounging on the stairs in a purple robe. He says that Shorty has run off with a Mexican girl to Louisiana and has left for good. I see Evelyn on the stairway. Her eyes are crazy, her face white. I think she has been crying, so I lay my hand on her shoulder. I have been a wife myself, and even a racist wife like this one should be comforted a little in the midst of the pay-back of her bad karma when her husband leaves home. But she is rigid, she pulls back. I guess you heard about Shorty, she says, that he left with a Mexican girl. Well, this isn't the end of it, she says, he's done it before, he'll be back, he's always back, dragging his tail, but I've had it myself. When he comes back this time, I won't have him anymore.

So he just left all of his apartments, I say.

Oh they're not his apartments, she says. He's always saying they're his, but they're not. He's just the manager, that's all. Now that he's gone, the owner says I can't stay here anymore.

But Shorty doesn't come back. Julian becomes the manager. He paints the office purple and white, and takes down the list of rules in the lobby. The minister from across the hall moves out, and three lesbians move in who shout and fight all night. The doors of the apartments stay open, rock and roll blaring out, people knocking at the door asking for a place to buy a lid, Evelyn moving out finally with her canaries. I see her some days later, her gray-brown hair loose around her face. It is a good day, lots of Dallas sun. She is carrying a grocery bag across the field in back of Tom Thumb Supermarket in a shortcut path across the block to Swiss Avenue, holding the hand of one of her blond-haired grand-daughters, a black man carrying a six-pack some paces on the path behind her, the weeds grown high with yellow flowers, the three of them picking their way in a small procession across the field.

▲▲▲▲▲▲

LEAPING
LEO

when you're down and out in Dallas you are down and out

—fr. de Dallas blues

In Dallas Leo is always working one place and I am working another. I get up in the morning while he's still in bed or after he's already gone to work, hours and days erratic working temporary jobs. I walk through the alley in back of our apartment house in the morning to Gaston Avenue to catch the bus to wherever Kelly Girl Services say I go, the exhaust fumes flooding over the curbs and crashing in rush-hour waves against the darkening brick mix of apartments/tattoo-parlor/Mex-Tex-bars/and fast-foods on both sides of the street. Leo coaxes the pickup truck to his jobs. He's registered with Manpower, Atlas, and Peak-Load, he loads Gatorade and drives a delivery route and makes electric circuit boards and sprays paint on pipes. And he comes home telling stories, you know how the newspaper said that street guy fell into downtown traffic and was killed? he tells me. Well, he didn't fall, he was pushed, that's what one of the men down at Atlas told me today. He was a purse snatcher and the cops couldn't catch him, so they finally pushed him under the wheels. And he tells me where some of the men sleep, under the freeway, and where they told him to go on the highway to ask truckers for work unloading in town, little pieces of labor pool lore, who's hiring where, and how many at a time. He works for two or three days at a time, then lays off for two or three days, sitting around in the efficiency apartment watching TV in his shorts, drinking beers, letting the aluminum cans pile up in grocery bags under the kitchen window, writing poems about how workers hate working and how he wishes he was alone and free and unencumbered and somewhere else.

In the evenings when I get off work, Leo and I sometimes walk down Gaston Avenue to Tom Thumb Supermarket, which is a grocery store, like the neighborhood, built in more peaceful, more affluent, tree-lined times for the sweet-stay-at-home-housewives who were our mothers, who abandoned these city neighborhoods for the safer cleaner Dallas north suburbs. Now it is sticky floors, broken glass in the crowded aisles, votive candles and mountain-pass cans of chile across from won-ton wrappers, strong-smelling men in Salvation Army suits cruising with grocery carts full of plastic-sacked beans and boxed rice, iron bars between the store doors and the parking lot to keep the carts from getting ripped off by grocery-bagged walkers. The store sits at the end of a horseshoe mall, but the dimestores and baby-knitting-fabric shops that once must have lined the other two sides of the parking lot are long gone, windows boarded up, one corner ex-drugstore now Mario's Lounge, with black plywood across the window glass, low-riders parked in front, young Chicanos lounging against the chrome-nosed hoods at night, Mario's door open and loud music coming out. One night at the supermarket checkout stand I am so happy to be off work for the day, so happy to be with Leo, who is holding my hand, I say Isn't this romantic, the two of us here checking out groceries, and Leo looks at me like I am crazy. You've got to be kidding, he says, no romanticism left in Leo anymore. He can see very clearly where he is, and it's no place good.

Because the truth is that the landscapes of Leo's memory/mind are like a series of snapshots from a family album. There are rolling green lawns of suburban homes and university campuses and country lots, and there is a family standing together on the front steps of a tidy home or in front of a tidy Christmas tree or lined up on the sides of a tidy turkey dinner: a small-boned beautiful angel-faced wife and two angel-boy-babies calling him Leo instead of Daddy in the liberal Unitarian style, while he points out nature to them in the ravines and hills of the paradise of nuclear family life in which they are growing up. So Leo's present reality dances across the stage in front of these green landscapes like a wino reeling his way through a Montessori School, hey where *are* we? Just where the hell are we? Wife, children, house and car, all gone, university job finally taken away for all the scandal and chaos that once kicked up like chicken feathers in a whing-a-ding transformation from Leo-the-professor to Leo-the-man falling falling falling for a shady woman with teenaged children (me) and poetry as a way of life. Somehow or another it has all come to this: Leo creating the plot of his own story from labor pool lounge to Tom Thumb barrio-market and seeing (incredibly!) himself in the faces of the other men there, too old, too poorly educated, too alcoholic, too suicidal, too lonely to be anything like him, but there they are anyway, wheeling the aisles of Tom Thumb together at

123

night and in the daytime sharing the same set of folding chairs.

Now if Leo didn't love me, he could be a poet and live alone in a cardboard box (like a man Leo read about in the *Dallas Morning News* who lived somewhere up east) and then he wouldn't have to work very much at all. He could simply eat cheap mackerel and soda crackers and write poetry all day. Or if I were simply myself alone, then we could be gypsies together, we could ride the rails and hitchhike and explore deserts and mountains and meet South American shaman and learn universal secrets from listening to the grass sing across the Canadian tundras and from kundalini-fucking in the dry bed of the Rio Grande. But I never seem to be myself alone, that sharp thin blade of a female fantasy-companion fit for a gypsy-poet-man. I always seem instead to have these children tying me to the world of work. In Dallas at first there is only one of these children, only Morgani, who is a grown child and works at a car wash bringing in one-third of the rent every month. But then there are two others, calling long distance from El Paso to say they no longer want to live with their father, wanting to come to Dallas for the school year and live with me. And I am a mother, born under the sign of Mother, called by the name of Mother and all of its variations wheeling off three children's developing tongues: the continuing chorus of all my adult years. So because of these children wanting to come, I think, well, we've got to be somewhere, we've got to have a place to sleep at least, the word *we* no longer meaning Leo and me, having wider and weightier implications.

Leo thinks maybe he will get a grant of money. But he doesn't. And then he thinks maybe someone rich will give him some money for the sake of poetry, but nobody does. And then he thinks maybe if we take off in the camper for two weeks in July for the annual-naked-hippie-Rainbow-Family gathering we will get a revelation, and some new kind of future other than temporary labor pools and Dallas apartment-semimigrant-neighborhoods will open up. We do go to the Rainbow-Family gathering, all right. But it rains, we only have wet wood and don't know how to build a fire, we get diarrhea, the wind blows toilet paper from the shitter around our tent poles, the tent falls down around our ears. So we're back in Dallas and poorer than we were before. I start looking around for a bigger place with a lease that allows children because it's already August and the school year is about to begin and my children are coming.

So one day I tell Leo, there is an apartment for rent just three doors down big enough for everybody.

How much a month?

Three hundred and twenty five, I say.

And he says, Utilities?

We pay them.

Well, that's over a hundred dollars more a month than what we're paying now.

I'll pay more than you need to, to cover the kids.

Who'll pay the deposit? he says.

Oh don't worry, I'll get it together. I lie-hope-wish-dream, because there's no more than fifty dollars in the envelope underneath the rug in the closet where I keep my money, and Kelly Girl Services hasn't called me for work in over four days. Leo looks at me like he knows I am lying and he is mad as hell but he isn't saying anything, because he's seen again that I am not alone, even though I try every night to make him forget it by making him concentrate on that singular body under the covers, but the truth is always there below the surface: Leo is working in labor pools in Dallas instead of crab-fishing on the Acapulco-Tibetan-desert-beach because the woman he has chosen is always shadowed by children not even his own.

This toward the end of the summer to beat all summers, July murdering grass and shrubs, August murdering babies, old people stroking and dying, burnt-out trees like torches outside the apartment window dead green and still. It is too hot to wear clothes, so I am hanging around the apartment with nothing on but a white half-slip pulled up to

125

my armpits. In the corner of the kitchen is a pile of used carpet that someone brought home from a dumpster because it is perfectly good. So I lie down on top of that and look out the window at nothing like a floundered fish pining for my kids because they're so good and I'm so bad, singing that old bad mother song. And Oh these kids, I think, they've been through shit with me, I quit their bankrupt ad-agency boozing dad thinking for sure I could make something better for us than that, but where am I now, baby, where am I now? My arm is over my eyes as I listen to Leo running bathwater on the other side of the wall, and I start to cry because I'm living in a two-room efficiency apartment in an East Dallas neighborhood where the winos piss in the park bushes across from the elementary school and I don't have a job and I don't even have a place for my kids to stay. And I don't even have a place for them to stay! Oh, I should have bought hose, I should have lacquered my fingernails and put my papers in a briefcase and finished my degree and copied my resumé and stopped pretending to be a writer, and I should have married someone other than Loe who could give me money anytime I asked for it, or stayed married to the children's dad who has become successful-sober-and-dull without me around, or I should have never moved to Dallas, I should have stayed in the country and gone to work in Wills Point for Champion Mobile Homes or at the local Dairy Queen dishing ice cream.

The front door opens, and it is Morgani in from the car wash. He comes into the kitchen and opens the refrigerator, but doesn't say anything to me probably thinking I am sleeping, with my arm over my face. And thank god thank god, I think, at least a little money comes in from Morgani, thank god for a grown son, oh, and I keep lying on that pile of carpet, not only am I not able to take care of my own children, I am not able to take care of *myself*! Here I am, no better than a fat black-shawled peasant mother being taken care of by a grown son. I am getting lower and lower—how can this be when I am such a *smart* person? How can such a bright-young-looking-kind-of-woman-for-her-age, such a—I would even say—sometimes *sexy* woman—who at the same time writes funny things as well as serious things, who is sometimes somewhat of a female folklore scholar, how can such a charismatic person be so *down and out?*

The telephone rings and Leo answers. He comes into the kitchen a few minutes later. He looks his worst, his arms and legs look skinny, his hair looks stringy. When he looks at me I hear him saying you-limpbag-of-depression-and-doldrums-you-witch-bitch, and when I look at him he can hear me saying you moneyless-no-good-bummer-nonpoet-of-a-man . . .

That was Grey Eagle on the telephone, he tells me, he's going to come over and drive us to his house so we can see some slides he took of the Rainbow Gathering. I think Oh no, oh no, not Grey Eagle, not the Rainbow Gathering, why oh why did I ever go to the naked-hippie-Rainbow-Family Gathering this summer in West Virginia, why did I let Leo talk me into spending my money on that? So I don't say anything. I just lie there with my arm on my eyes.

Leo says so do you want to go?

No.

He says I think you should go, I think you should get out of this apartment.

So I take my arm down but don't look at him. I look around for my shoes. I'll go I say, reaching around for the pants I had on that are somewhere.

Just then someone knocks at the door and Morgani answers it, and it is my biker-brother passing through El Paso on his way to Dallas, who gave one of my kids a ride. So I hug this particular kid, who is blond and sixteen, and I tell him that he looks good, because he does, and we walk out of the kitchen into the other room. He says, so this is it, huh? And I say yes, this is it.

Where am I going to sleep?

And I wave to the floor and say, here for right now.

Where's the other kid going to sleep when she comes?

And I say, she's going to sleep here, too.

My biker-brother sits down on the couch, red beard frazzled, face red, Leo brings him a beer.

This city is already freaking me out, my biker-brother says, I don't see how you can stand living in the middle of the city. I called out to your house in the country first thinking you'd be there. Some other people had your number. They said they had people calling for you all the time.

We haven't been out there for a long time, I say. For one thing, our truck's on its last legs, so Leo has only been using it to drive to jobs.

I don't know why you don't live out there anymore, my biker-brother says.

Well, we're not living out there because we ran out of money and there wasn't any work, I say.

Oh you could have worked if you wanted to, Leo says.

Where?

You never even asked around.

Well, at any rate it certainly seemed to me that there wasn't any way to make a living there.

Someone knocks on the door again, and this time it is Grey Eagle. Leo introduces Grey Eagle to my biker-brother and they shake hands. On one side of the handshake is Grey Eagle, whose beard is grey and whose cheeks are rosy from hippie vitality, who lives by himself on bee pollen and rose hips, who looks like Leo himself might look if he were fifty and lived alone, and on the other side of the handshake is my biker-brother full of biker blood lust, his face already dark red from homicidal city vibes. Leo asks my biker-brother if he wants to come see slides of the Rainbow Gathering. My biker-brother says yes, and we leave the apartment with Morgani and the other kid sharing a joint. We drive to Grey Eagle's ranch-style house with trimmed-up bushes in a quiet North Dallas neighborhood. He sets up his carousel slide projector on a coffee table in the living room and starts projecting larger-than-lifesize photographs of two nude blond women, one a well-preserved forty, the other in her teens. These are mother and daughter, he says, who came to Dallas from New

128

Mexico and convoyed with me to the hippie Rainbow Gathering the rest of the way. I took these shots of them in the shower the night they were staying here. We were just goofing around.

Now that's quite a mother, my biker-brother says.

The older woman lathers the younger woman's boobs for several slides in a row, then for several others the two of them change places.

I wouldn't mind some of that ass, my biker-brother says.

These are my Rainbow sisters, Grey Eagle says like a gentle reprimand.

Jesus, look at those tits, my biker-brother says.

Grey Eagle picks up the pace, clicks through five or six fast glimpses of blond pubic hair and smiles and stoops and bends. Then the blond women are suddenly replaced with panoramas of nude women bathing in streams, hiking along forest trails holding hands, eating fruit, carrying babies, everyone looking free from the cities, from working, for the taking, for Grey Eagle or my biker-brother or Leo, anyone who can claw through the screen. My biker-brother is going crazy. He is drinking up Grey Eagle's red wine, he is talking cunt and tits, so Grey Eagle shuts off the slides and turns to him. If you're going to talk like that about the Rainbow sisters, he says, I won't be able to show you the slides.

Leo has been sitting on the floor not saying anything, drinking one long-neck Lone Star after another, but now he speaks up. Well you do show more photographs of nude women than you do nude men, he says, although maybe it's natural if you're a man to have that bias, and his words are thick but precise.

I want to see some more of the shower girlies, my biker-brother says.

The thing is, Grey Eagle says, these people let me take these photographs because they know me, they know I'd never hurt them in any way.

Oh I'd never hurt them either, my biker-brother says,

129

oh maybe I'd want to fuck them but I wouldn't want to hurt them.

Well they know that we are like brother and sister, Grey Eagle says.

Or maybe I would only hurt them a little, my biker-brother says, if they hurt me or something like that.

Grey Eagle turns off the slide projector.

Well, I guess it's time to take us back, I say. So we're back in the car, I sit in the front seat with Grey Eagle, Leo and my biker-brother in the back seat. We drive back the way we came, through the quiet winding streets of North Dallas to the freeway back south toward downtown. Grey Eagle tells me maybe I should write a story, maybe I should write something about women who work for the railroads and he could take the photographs and we could make some money collaborating that way. A Mercedes whizzes past, and my biker-brother throws the driver a finger and yells Fuck you! out the window. Another car passes and he throws them a finger, too, and yells fuck you! fuck you! Then Leo starts throwing fingers out the back window at the car behind us. I see him fluttering his fingers in and out of his ears, and Grey Eagle says or maybe we could do a story together about women who work for the highway department fixing roads. Leo is yelling You rich bastard! You rich filth!

And Grey Eagle pulls up to the curb in front of our apartment, and my biker-brother says, Trisha stays calm through everything, she runs the show.

There is a pause, and then Leo says, yes, she does run the show, doesn't she?

Then he slams out of the car and runs up the apartment steps and disappears. My biker-brother gets out with a happy booze smile on his face. He is swaying back and forth holding the last of a gallon bottle of red wine he took from Grey Eagle's house and one of Grey Eagle's glasses. I wave to Grey Eagle as he pulls away from the curb. My biker-brother puts his arm around me, I love you, he says, because you're always running the show.

When we walk into the apartment Leo is throwing clothes, books, and papers into a duffel bag. I am leaving here! he yells when he hears the door open, and I never want to see any of your faces again! He walks out, slams the door. Morgani and the other kid are sitting on the couch watching TV, hardly look up when Leo walks out the door. Maybe we don't want to see him again either, Morgani says.

Well he must love you, my biker-brother says. He probably left so that he wouldn't beat you up.

So Leo walks out the apartment to Gaston Avenue where the buses run, but before he gets on a bus he walks down to Mario's Lounge and gets *really* drunk. And then afterward he gets his suitcases stolen while he's waiting for the bus. And he heads for Austin where his ex-nurse-wife is living with the children who at least are his own. But I don't know any of this until he calls me the next night from the nurse-wife's phone. Why don't you come down to Austin? he says. You could work Kelly Girl Services down here. But I say no.

Two days later he calls again, and he's now in Galveston as a poet-in-the-schools living in a camper truck because he happened to walk into the right office at the right time. Why don't you come down to Galveston? he says. But the ocean is behind him and the seagulls are swooping down on his shoulders and back up and down again and calling, and the beach is all sand and no rocks, and Leo is already dancing with the Galveston dancers and singing to the blond sisters who are not yet mothers in the Galveston bars, Leo unencumbered as light itself since Gaston Avenue took all his papers and clothes.

131

▲▲▲▲▲▲

SERMON
ON
THE
RAT

This story is dedicated to my ex-brother-in-law Angelo's stepfather
(called by his family Joe-De-Rat) who weighs 300 lbs. and has a
disability and stays home and whose wife, who is Angelo's mother,
Annie, continues to live with him and make spaghetti for him for love
of the Catholic Church and other dark reasons of her own.

Sometime in the not-too-far past this neighborhood has been
taken over by a certain line of outside cats big as raccoons.
Once I see two out my window loping across the vacant lot

132

on the other side of the street like they are bringing antelopes down. These cats are everywhere—they don't seem to have particular houses, they just have the neighborhood, and some of them take over whole backyards. There is one backyard just a few doors down with a bathtub on the front lawn full of flowers and a backyard where there must be forty cats, every one of them black, so that it must be some black cat staked that territory out years ago and now all his descendants are still there, holding their inheritance. Black mothers loll under the bushes nursing black babies, and black cats big as boxers sit on their hind legs watching out for suspicious street traffic. A yardful of yellow eyes watches me when I walk along although they aren't at all like dogs, as you probably know, because they could care less who comes walking along just so long as it's nothing good to eat and displays no danger signs, because they're enjoying just lying around in their cat herd.

I try to keep a little black one in my apartment because he is so incredibly beautiful. I feed him canned food and milk and share my meals with him, but as soon as he gets big he goes off anyway. I see him in the vacant lot sometimes, twice and then three times bigger. I wonder why did he leave? I fed him better than any cat I ever had, and I wonder what and where he could find anything better to eat. I really do think about this question from time to time when I spot him or those other cats, so sleek and huge, by god eating something that makes them the biggest cats I have ever seen.

But it does not dawn on me what sirloin tip caught on the run and eaten hot these pussies eat to stay fit until I move from my efficiency apartment to a two-story duplex down the street, with weeds knee high in the front lawn and a garage in the back full of junk. I rent the second floor because it will sleep me and three kids if we put beds in the dining room, because it has a balcony overlooking the street and because for its size it is cheap. Now why is it so cheap? I figure that part of the reason is that the building needs paint, the columns supporting the balcony are cracked and the yard is generally run down. And then Leroy the landlord doesn't want any hassle, he says. He doesn't ask much deposit, he doesn't make me sign a lease, but he says I shouldn't call him about little troubles, and he makes it clear that little troubles include just about everything short of the building burning down.

Do you have a dog, he asks. I say no, and he says, Well that's good because dogs shed so much. And do you have cats? I say no. And he says well, you might think about getting one, they're always good to keep the mice down. I don't think too much about that until I start cleaning the kitchen cabinets and find a spring trap about a foot long, large enough to cripple a horse. Sure enough, as soon as I turn out the lights the first night in the apartment, a party begins in the walls. The squealing and scurrying and scuffling is so loud that I try to translate what I'm hearing. Are they quarreling in there? Are they fucking? Are babies being born?

The next evening my daughter Pearl starts supper in the kitchen. She suddenly screams and when I come to see what is going on she is sitting at the table wide-eyed and shaken.

I saw a rat this long, she says, she spreads her arms out wide, running along there. She points to a hot water pipe close to the ceiling.

Are you sure it wasn't a mouse?

She says it was a rat.

Are you sure it was that big?

She says it was at least that big, maybe it was bigger.

So she doesn't want to be left alone in the kitchen anymore, and I don't either, although I still haven't seen anything myself yet, except for rat turds that I find every morning when I want to fix breakfast all over the cans and boxes in the pantry like a black hailstorm hits in there every night. I keep cleaning the rat turds away and finding them again when I open the door and cleaning them away and finding them again until I finally say to myself Enough is enough! So I get a cabinet that looks all right from the garage and bring it upstairs into the kitchen and put all my pantry goods in that. I shut the pantry door and nail the very large rat trap I found earlier to the middle of the door. Above and below the rat trap I paint in purple and black large letters:

DIS IS
DE RAT'S HOUSE
KNOCK BEFORE
ENTERING

The idea being, of course, that if you knock he'll scurry away and you don't have to see him. So when friends come over if they say something about the door, I demonstrate how it works. I knock, I open the door and they look at all the rat turds, which I don't clean up anymore, and they say polite half-hesitant kinds of things like they're not really sure if this is art or not, and then usually they don't say anything else about it.

Now downstairs lives my Yankee neighbor Simon-Polli, once a European refugee kid come to Illinois with his father, now in Texas talking like he owns the place. Sometimes he visits to smoke a joint or drink a cup of coffee, and periodically the subject of the rats will come up. Simon says that we should work together getting rid of the rats. He is putting out poison but if I don't do it too his poison won't have any effect. He is also putting out traps, but if I don't put out traps his traps won't make any difference. And I know I am subjecting myself to such labeling as *stupid, sentimental, careless* and *naive,* but I can't put down traps and I can't buy poison and I tell him so. I make this a joke one night: I read in a book, I tell him, that you can get rid of rats by writing to them. You just write a letter and tell them why they should leave your place and where they should go, give them specific instructions. So I could say, dear rats:

Simon downstairs is putting all this poison out
and upstairs I never have much around for you to
eat anyhow
so what you should do immediately

135

is go to the dumpster in back of Tom Thumb
        Supermarket
which is five blocks east and one block south
where you will find mounds of delicious
overripe and half-rotten edibles
mixed right for rats

sincerely and with personal concern
Pat Ellis Rat-Writer

So after you write the letter, you roll it up, tie it with a string, grease it down, stick it in a rat hole and the rat eats it, see, he digests your words.

But Simon doesn't think this is funny nor feasible. Well Pat, he says, you tell me when you're ready to do something real because it isn't going to do that much good unless we work together.

So have you caught any?

Sure I have, he says.

How many?

I've caught about half a dozen, he says.

(Half a dozen! That many dead and still so much squealing and scurrying in the walls!)

Well, I tell him, I'm thinking about it a lot, I am really thinking about it.

I mean you don't screw around about rats, they carry bubonic plague, fleas, all kinds of diseases.

I tell him I am aware of that. I don't know why I'm defending the rats. But then I don't know whether I can kill rats and still be a good vegetarian or if blood lust for rats might someday bar me from hippiehindu heaven, and the philosophical questions these rats raise keep me from spending what little money I have after covering the basics on poison and traps and other armaments of rat war, preferring instead to spend on personal pleasure.

Just wait till you see one of these rats, Simon says, how big they really are, then your head will clear up fast.

The first rat I see is behind the refrigerator. I only see his tail. I think it is a rope at first or part of an electrical cord, but then it moves. The second rat I see is at first a sound that wakes me up at night and then when I raise up I see or think I see a dark shape in the middle of the floor running from one end of the room to the other. Then finally one evening I really see one. I use a sliding door for a wall at the end of my room, and in front of it is my file cabinet where I put my purse after work, and this one evening there is an apple in my purse that I had brought for my lunch but hadn't eaten. Sometime in the night I hear noises coming from that direction. I turn on the light and there is a louder noise but I don't see anything. So I turn the light back off. As soon as I turn off the light, the noise starts up, and it sounds too loud and immediate to be inside the wall. There is a thump and a scrape and a roll, and when I turn the light back on there is a *rat* poking his head out of the crack where the sliding door goes into the wall, and in his front paws is my apple. For an infinite moment we look at each other—me on an elbow, eyes wide, one hand still on the lamp switch, he with his head sideways sticking out of the wall, little ears, little bright eyes, little paws around the apple. Then the wall is suddenly blank again, apple and rat inside it. And this was a big apple! A big red delicious.

Now in the past and up to this time, I have seen glimpses of rats sometimes, sometimes dead or scurrying or laboratory trapped, and sometimes I have seen rat pictures and read about rats in stories and have generally breathed in the rat myth-image we Westerners tend to share: the plague rat (like Simon says) who brings death to our homes and chews through the dignity of our coffins if we don't line them well enough, and eats our bodies up. But I have never had a rat-vision like this one: the grey face and round ears, peering over the red apple, suspended sideways in a moment of still curiosity halfway up the white sliding door, then the sudden disappearing act. And I'm struck half blind by this revelation for the rest of the night, charmed by a rat rather than vice-versa. He has written me a letter in one long look. He has told me he won't pay a bit of attention to directions for the supermarket dump, there's no sense in that. He knows there's a jungle outside these house walls, he knows better than anybody what keeps those outside cats so fat. Besides, he's lived here for years raising family after family, his ancestors were here when Dallas wasn't, when this was a forest instead of a house. But he doesn't mind sharing space with me because he's a vegetarian himself and likes my habits. He likes my apples, he likes my granola crumbs, he likes my marijuana; in fact, he has had some grand revelations during his writhings weathering Simon's strychnīne out of his system. He himself has seen a time when rats and people will be willing to live peacefully together in the same house. And he leaves his signature with his lightning exit:

> Rat Ellis Taylor
> *author of sounds and turds from*
> *the other*
> *side*

▲▲▲▲▲▲

NEWS
FROM
EL
CORAZON:
IN
THE
COMPOSING
ROOM

We all know how Sleazy Street is
it's up in the mornings with too many kids
it's too many men coming in the back door
and not enough time to sweep the floor
it's coffee in the pot and a dirty sugar spoon
it's towels on the floor of a dirty bathroom
and a smell like me and a smell like you
all mixed together in a Sleazy Street stew
Sleazy Street stew, oh Sleazy Street stew
it smells like me and it smells like you
gimme gimme gimme that Sleazy Street stew

—especially composed for Pauline
Footloose & Hr 5-piece Baby-Band

Leo says of course we will get together again. He calls me long distance from Seven-Eleven parking lots and says that he loves me and he sends me a hundred dollars a month to keep his name on the mailbox, he in fact spends great parts of his poet-in-the-schools money to drive from Galveston to Dallas for weekends of lovemaking and whispered reassurances and barbequed chicken crowded around the little kitchen table with me and the three kids like he is simply a commuting husband and this family is really his. At first he comes almost every weekend and his hundred-dollar share of the rent comes on the first of the month. But as fall wears into winter he doesn't visit so much, and the money still comes but it comes later and later, too late to cover the rent, so that by spring I realize that I have got to stop counting on it, the rent is going to have to come from me. Me the sometimes writer. Me the newborn bookstore clerk. And me the mother with the asset of Morgani the working son. He does pay his part of the rent, too. So the household lurches along paying its bills on minimum wage and money that sometimes appears in the mail—homages to love from Leo and occasional checks from newspaper accounting offices rewarding me for using my time to write commercially viable articles on choosing melons in the supermarket and growing indoor palms, instead of wasting my skills on stories and poems that do not sell.

But life is not grim. I like this upstairs apartment I find myself in. Even with rats in the walls and weeds in the driveway, it has its advantages. There is a room for each of us, and my kids are electronic age kids, so each room has its own kind of electrical noise: Second Son playing stereo, Daughter playing radio, son Morgani playing electric guitar, playing the loudest and longest, wanting to be a rock musician so he won't have to work at the car wash anymore, so that he practices his guitar all the time. But the rooms are big and separated from each other because of a central hall, so it is only at certain peak times of voltage overload that I finally have to let out some kind of yell or scream or politely pointed question: would you please turn it down? This never stops the mix of noise for good of course, only long enough to give a

140

little quiet time in the evening, a little peace, so my head can come to rest and my thoughts settle down before the sound level builds up again.

Best of all features in this apartment is a white door in my bedroom, a magical device. The kids can be rocking and rolling, shouting jokes at each other through the walls, they can be trundling the bicycle up the stairs and down the stairs and bringing home friends to play pool on the pool table we found in the alley and placed in Second-Son's room, and all I have to do is to open this door in my bedroom and step outside. Just like that the lights are out. The electronic noise is far behind me. I am standing on a second-story balcony supported on crumbling columns and embraced in the clutch of massive oak branches surrounding the upper part of the house. In the daytime I am in the company of blue jays who soar down through the leaves, and squirrels running the branches, and at night I am in the company of stars. I can sit in my used-to-belong-to-Grandmaw rocker out there in the evening and put my feet up on a nail barrel I use for both table and stool and turn my own little radio to the country-and-western station none of my kids can stand listening to and smoke a joint. Oh, sing it Dolly! Listen to the man play that fiddle! I look down through the tree branches at the cars and bicycles and people passing on the street below who rarely look up long enough to spot me in the leaves—the Vietnamese grandmother who comes down the sidewalk every morning with her cluster of children collecting cans, the black man with the twenty braids and red ribbons who rides his bicycle every day, the regular joggers and the dog walkers, the couples shouting angry words at each other while they walk, and the couples with arms around each other, the Friday night drunks and the Saturday morning whistling mailman. I study them like I study the pigeons who prance and flutter through their various bird rituals along the roof-top of the house next door, composing stories for each one of them, and, like a benevolent director, assigning them roles I imagine them performing off-stage out of porch range.

In the apartment downstairs lives Simon-Polli. When

I first take up my observation post on the balcony, I see his comings and goings on the walk below me with an array of thin, young and lacquered women on his arm. He is enrolled in the downtown community college, with plans for becoming an accountant/male model and masseur, and he says that the electric guitar playing above his desk keeps him from studying very well. Morgani learns to turn the decibels down when Simon-Polli knocks a broom handle against the ceiling. I don't like Simon-Polli too much, I don't like his black pompadour and little twitchy mustache, and I don't like the endless photographs in the Simon-Polli portfolio he wants to show me with every invitation to his apartment for a beer—Simon-Polli lounging in bikini trunks on a broken brick wall, Simon-Polli dressed in a black gypsy outfit smoldering at the camera eye, closeups of Simon-Polli with his nostrils flared and his pores open. But I do occasionally like to hear his stories. So when he stands in the front yard waving a poorly rolled joint looking up at me on my balcony perch, I sometimes invite him up to sit with me in the branches. Simon-Polli came from Eastern Europe somewhere. His earliest photographs, he says, showed him as a skinny kid with a shaved head symbol of lice control standing in front of a tent in a refugee camp with his father because when they were released from the concentration camp where his mother died there was no place for what remained of his family to go. He spent five years after the war going from one camp to another, traveling on trains that stopped in towns and villages where constables blocked the doors so that no refugees could get off. Then finally to America with a handful of family jewels that his father parlayed into a decent living selling used cars in Chicago. I don't know why Simon-Polli came to Dallas. That is one of the mystery stories he doesn't tell. To go to a community college to study massage? That's what he says.

Simon-Polli has a European sentimental streak at least as strong as that streak in me that keeps my radio tuned to the country-and-western station. His eyes get teary when he talks about his father. He fulminates about the coldness other students exhibit toward him in the college halls. At times he grabs his guitar and brings it up to the balcony with him and croons out oily love songs from Dean Martin albums to the passing joggers. One evening he comes with his guitar, full of emotion.

I'm going to be a father again, he says, my four-year-old son is coming from New York to stay with me because his mom doesn't want him anymore.

Well, I didn't even know he had a son or an ex-wife, but I say Wow Simon, that sounds pretty exciting.

I wrote a song, he says, I'm going to sing it for my son when he gets off the airplane. Then Simon starts singing—Oh Mathias, I love you, you are the sky's blue, you are a bird of a beautiful hue, my son, my Mathias—Simon-Polli sings with his eyes closed, his lips pursed up to the moon above the balcony like a Jewish coyote.

The son does come, and is the most scowling, worried, and mean little kid I have ever seen. He has thick black eyebrows that meet in a permanent seam between his eyes. For the sake of good neighbor relations and in exchange for Simon's not complaining too much about my own noisy kids, I agree to babysit the son from time to time for free. This in fact does make Simon very happy. He invites me to come down anytime I want to smoke grass with him, from his stash box kept full by generous checks from his father in Chicago.

One evening I'm sitting out on my balcony when I see Simon-Polli coming up the front walk carrying a large over-stuffed chair, followed by Mathias, who is picking up little rocks and throwing them at his father's ankles.

Cut it out! Simon is shouting.

No! Mathias is shouting back.

When Simon sees me he calls up. See this great chair? I bought it from this lady down the street who's being evicted. It's okay, it's got some broken springs. She was asking seventy-five but I talked her into taking fifteen.

Sounds like a bargain, I say.

Oh, I just felt sorry for her, not that I wanted the chair, he says. Although it looks okay, just the springs are a little bad.

143

Mathias lobs another stone.

I said cut it out! Simon shouts.

I said no! Mathias shouts.

They go in. There is the sound of whopping and screaming and crying, and I look up the street in the direction the two of them came from to see what is going on. Sure enough, I see Daughter standing with some more kids around a pile of stuff along the curb about six houses down. The sun, I also notice, is almost gone. I lean across the balcony rail and call down the street for Daughter to come home. She comes running. In a minute she's on the balcony. There's a girl with her about the same height, long brown hair like hers, same budding build with almost-boobs making little bumps under her blouse and hips gathered ready to begin making curves.

This is Fran, Daughter says, she's fourteen, her family's the one that's being evicted.

Hello, Fran says, the same as if Daughter had said Fran's family owned every house on the block.

Hello, I say, do y'all have a place to sleep tonight?

Fran frowns a little bit. Oh, I don't know yet. My mom is trying to call some people. She starts squinting down the sidewalk back at the pile of stuff on the curb. I better go back and see what my little sister is doing.

Well, you tell your mom you can sleep on the floor here tonight, I tell her, if nothing else turns up.

I'm thinking that blankets thrown down for them on a bare floor in the apartment of strangers isn't much, they will have to be pretty desperate to accept an offer like that. But if they don't know where they're staying yet, when it's already dark, then they must all feel pretty scared, and any invitation is better than the prospect of no beds for the night. So Daughter and Fran run back down the stairs and onto the sidewalk. The streetlamps are on, and I can see a pickup truck with its door open parked along the side of the pile. There's a black man leaning on the side of it, and some little kids playing around the pile. Then Fran and Daughter are there, standing, talking, but too far away for me to get what's going on. I am in the kitchen washing the dishes when Daughter and Fran come back. You need to talk to her mom, Daughter says, but they don't know yet where they'll be staying.

So I stop the water and walk down with the two girls. The black man is still leaning on the truck. He is watching two men speaking loud Spanish to each other. One holds up a pair of pants from the pile to himself and laughs, and the other nods his head up and down like those pants fit him just right, and there is this little blond woman tottering around the two men on tiny three-inch spike heels made out of clear plastic, wearing a white nylon skirt like she just got finished drinking daiquiris at some country club, pointing her finger emphatically, saying Put that down! You put that down!

Hey man, put that down, I say while I'm walking up. When he doesn't, I tap my chest a couple of times and say, A little heart man, a little *corazón*—Corazón, I say, close up to him, clenching my fist and shaking it over my heart. This is a Chicano charm I learned in El Paso, since *corazón* is something no good Mexican man ever wants to be caught short of. Sure enough he puts it down and the two of them snicker, swagger away, saying things I don't try to translate, and the little woman picks up the pants from the sidewalk and tries to fold them up. I was just telling your daughter, I say to her, that if you didn't have a place to stay you could come stay at our place for the night.

Oh! She's all full of emotion suddenly, shaking my hand. Didn't I tell you? she asks the black man, who has been leaning on the truck in the same position through the whole encounter. The Lord provides. And I don't correct her there, we will resort to abstracts like that the rest of the night to cover up our shyness at this strange situation: stranger asks other strangers to move into her house, a city act as strong as street sex, more easily talked about when veiled in euphemism and depersonalized, so that Pauline isn't really Pauline but the voice that cried out, the one in need, the little lost lamb, so that Pat the person came down from her balcony and entered the story as the Lord and pushed the wheel of Pauline's crossed stars and wrote the address down for the next installment of Pauline's karma.

What are you going to do with all of this stuff, I ask her. She just looks puzzled, staring at all the pile of mattresses and black plastic bags, piles of clothes and shoes and papers already beginning to blow away. So I say, maybe you can put it all in my backyard for right now.

The black man suddenly unbends, smiles and says all *right*, like he's been waiting all this time for just those words. He starts throwing things into the back of the truck.

I'll go down and get my sons to help, I say, so I trot back to the house. Morgani's out, but Second Son is there and the two of us walk back to the truck. Pauline is running back and forth, up and down the sidewalk, first lifting a bag, putting it down, herding Fran and the little sister out of the way, talking in explosive sentence fragments.

He stole the television, she says, I'm going to sue him, she says, not suitable, she says, now that's the way he puts it, and look at this! She tucks her chin in at me and points over her shoulder, it took me three days to pack it all up.

Sure enough, I can see lots of things that have been put in black plastic bags are now half dumped, the tops of the bags coming untied. So we all start putting things on the back of the truck, and the black man drives the truck down the block and into our driveway where we unload it, and we do this two or three times until nothing is left on the sidewalk.

By this time it's about ten o'clock. The black man (whose name is Bennie and whose position in Pauline's story is never quite clear except that his truck has been made an instrument-of-god) wants a joint after we make the last load, and I tell him that I'm out but I'll go ask Simon my neighbor for one. So I knock on Simon's door. Simon's mustache is twitching over the chain latch on the second knock. I stick out my tongue and make a face like I'm all dogged out, which in fact I am.

We've just got finished moving a family upstairs, I tell him.

Oh no, he says, you moved that woman and her kids in with you that got evicted?

146

She didn't have a place to stay, it'll just be for a night or so, until she can figure it all out.

Oh no, he says, I don't mean to sound like a bastard, but I can't take it. She can't move in. There's agencies to take care of people like her. I'm about to go crazy, Pat, he says. I'm studying and having to get up early to take Mathias to day care. Shit.

Look, Simon, I say, it's just going to be for a little while. Listen, do you have a joint?

Bennie the black man has come up on the porch and is standing right behind me.

Simon looks over my shoulder significantly, then looks at me again. For you?

I smile, shrug, guilty as hell suddenly because I'm asking Simon for a joint for everyone.

You come down later, he says, I'll give you a joint anytime, but nothing for them.

Does he have any grass? Bennie asks me while Simon closes the door.

Not really, I say. Pauline shuffles up in her little high heel shoes, and we go upstairs. When we get to the top, there is Pauline, there is Bennie, there is Fran the teenage daughter and her little sister, but then there is another baby, too, one I've never seen before, and there is also a German shepherd and a little black puppy. Pauline looks apologetic.

This is Willy, she says, pointing to the strange baby boy, dirty faced, in dirty shorts, no more than two years old, slightly smaller than the baby sister.

So okay, I am thinking, there are three children, a woman and two dogs, but this wheel is set in motion now. They will only be here a few days, they really will not be here very long.

Someone carries up mattresses from the pile of stuff in the backyard, someone gets sheets, pillows. Morgani comes in with two joints he's gotten somewhere. So we sit down on Pauline's mattress and everybody smokes, even Willy the little baby-kid takes tokes like he's been doing it since he was born.

147

And we start talking about Dallas, whether we want to stay here or not. Bennie the black man says he wants to live in Dallas all his life and become a well-respected gangster, Morgani says he wants to be a rock musician but maybe somewhere else, and I don't say because I am too busy taking this new landscape in to think of another one. Daughter and Fran are already in Dreamland falling asleep together on the floor, and Willy the little boy-kid is walking around without his pants on, little baby penis peeking out from under round little baby belly. Full of marijuana, in the middle of marijuana talk with a big self-confident baby grin, taking for granted that it doesn't matter where he is, he owns it all.

▲

Of course, I say, it will only be one or two days, but it won't be just that, it will be one or two weeks or maybe it will be one or two months, even when I am moving the stuff into the backyard, even when I am talking to Simon downstairs, I know that saying one or two days is stupid. It is unrealistic. If a single person becomes down and out and gets evicted, then maybe it would only take one or two days to get things straightened out. But a woman with little children is something else again. First, this woman needs some money, she needs either welfare or a job. Then she needs to get herself a place to stay, and then she needs to get some day care for her little kids so that her big kid, Fran, now their all-the-time babysitter, can go to school. Welfare tells her they'll pay her rent for a house, but first she has to get one. Then they will need to inspect it and approve it and file papers on it, all of which takes about six weeks. So she either gets a job and saves her money and pays the rent for that time and the deposit, or she talks a landlord into waiting almost two months for his money. Where can she stay in the meantime? On the streets, at the Salvation Army, here with me.

Then there are other problems, there are the problems that made this elaborate system collapse in the first place. Pauline tells me these other problems in little pieces of sentences that tumble out while her eyes roll and her voice goes higher and faster with emotion. Pauline is scattered—she is a woman who has been under heavy fire and is freaking out. When I ask her a question the answer tends to be so complicated with names and events and history I've never heard of that I quickly lose track of what she is talking about. But she is very angry and when she finds out I am a writer, she thinks I will be able to tell the world what she is angry about. First, she wants to sue the landlord who kicked her out. She also wants to sue the landlord who kicked her out before that. And then she wants to expose the Texas Parole Board for not letting her old man out. An eight-year prison term, she says, is too long for burglary. Sometimes she tells me it was a first offense, bur sometimes she says he had been a thief, was always a thief, although she hadn't asked him about it, she didn't know. But these things, she says, that were up in her attic in Oak Cliff—the television sets and stereos and whatnot—they hadn't even been stolen by her old man, he had been framed, of course—they had been stolen by her *ex-*old man, who was in cahoots with their teenage son by that marriage (Fran's brother) who was now in juvenile prison himself, just like her old man, serving time.

This is the way they had it, she tells me. Her voice gathers low and intense for a slow build while she waves a pancake spatula over the skillet and I drink coffee, they had *me* in the newspaper as the head of some burglary ring in Oak Cliff! Me! And I didn't even know anything about it! Oh, we sold a little tape recorder because it was there, but what could we do? There it all was in the attic! And I told that police of-icer he was taking an innocent man, we had been framed by my *ex-*husband, who is a *fiend*, he is a *demon*, he is the devil him-self, laughing up his sleeve while we're spending time in jail. I even went to jail myself! For five days! She lifts Willy the boy-kid up onto the chair by the table. You want some pancakes?

And this ex-husband, she says, you don't know what he is like. He put a rifle down my throat, here I was nude, see, and he puts a rifle down my throat and says: *suck on this, bitch!* She glares at me with her jaw stuck out like it is him saying it. *Suck on this, bitch!* And there I was crawling out the bathroom window nude, bloody, because he beat me up—see, right here. She shows me some lumps on her head. So I was screaming for help *nude* at the door of some neighbor's.

I'm eating my pancakes, watching her act this all out. I'd like to know lots of details she's leaving out, but she's going too fast to stop, and I'll hear it all again anyway. She'll tell me over and over *suck on this, bitch!* She'll tell me exactly how he said it—*suck on this, bitch!*—until I have the story almost memorized just the way she tells it, with how she gets away left out, with how he got in left out, with what house it happened in left out, just the nude woman against the bathroom tile and the *ex*-old man putting the rifle in her mouth.

▲

Every morning Pauline gets up, gets herself together, and makes breakfast for the babies, and when she leaves she looks great. She is a trim little woman with lots of fluffy blond hair, who can make herself look like a perfect little doll when she puts on her job-hunting outfit and spends some careful time on her face in front of the bathroom mirror. She always wanted to be a model, she says, but this never quite got off the ground, although she shows me a certificate she once got in a 1961 Miss Teenage America Contest held in Fort Worth, and she wants to get enough money sometime to straighten Fran's teeth so that the daughter can be given more opportunities to be a model than her mother was. She does have some connections in the movies, her babies could be movie stars, they're so cute, if she could just get hold of this guy she used to know when he first started shooting film, but she thinks he's in California. In the meantime she throws the I Ching several times a day and gets conflicting answers, and goes by all of them, and changes her mind each time about what kind of job to get and where to live. She can do secretarial work, and in fact does get a job, but it only lasts two days. Then she gets another job doing telephone work, but it's at night and she can't work out the transportation. Then she gets another job and this lasts for a week before they lay her off, the cloud of Pauline's complications always quickly evident to any employer—a woman whose answers to the simplest questions are too complicated, who is already late or missing work the first days of the job because she has no adequate transportation and too many babies at home.

Fran babysits for her mother but doesn't like it. She calls her mother at work whenever she can, telling Pauline to talk to the babies on the telephone to make them behave. The babies like talking to Pauline but it doesn't make them any better. Although they aren't bad babies, they are simply babies, lively and into everything, and then maybe even livelier and happier than some because whatever problems Pauline might have, she nevertheless loves her babies and doesn't discipline them much, so they are lively healthy babies who have never been beaten up. And Fran has learned child care from her mother. She never hits them, she never hurts them, although she doesn't know what things to do to make them mind, sometimes simply becomes a baby herself, laughing and rolling with them on the floor. But then Pauline calls at five-thirty or six-thirty or seven and says she met a friend or stayed for a drink until rush hour was over and that she'll be home soon, and Fran hangs up the telephone and says Shit! Shit! and smokes cigarettes and yells at the babies and slams doors and drawers until Pauline comes home.

On Sundays Pauline has to decide if she'll take the Salvation Army bus to Huntsville to visit her husband-framed-by-her-ex or take the bus to Gainesville to be with her son in the juvenile prison. Fran is freaking out from babysitting, she babysits all week and doesn't want to babysit on the weekends, too, but Pauline leaves so early in the morning that Fran is still asleep and doesn't find out until she wakes up that she is babysitting again. Then whatever time her mother comes in, whether it's five o'clock in the evening or one o'clock at night, she runs out of the house. She drives around with the older boys in the neighborhood, she goes to the apartment houses where the older boys live to get high, to listen to records, to let them feel her up, whatever trade-off she can do just to get away from the babies for a little while and her mother. Pauline yells at her when Fran pushes past her, heading for whatever is out there. Where do you think you're going, young lady? she says.

Fran yells, Out!

Pauline yells, Well, you better be home in half an hour!

The door slams and Pauline comes into my room and sits on my bed. I just don't know what do with Fran, Pauline says.

Pauline, she's just babysitting too much, she's too young, she's bound to be freaking out.

Well, still, Pauline says, she shouldn't talk to her mother like that.

Daughter is glum. When Pauline leaves Daughter starts up—why can't I go with Fran? she asks me. I'm almost as old as she is, she invited me to go.

Daughter is sitting up in the middle of my bed pouting, a little lipstick and blue eye shadow on her face that Fran let her use and she's already looking like a young woman, but I don't care, I don't care, she's not old enough to be in this story Fran's beginning to plot out. Look, I tell her, you've seen those gangs of men on the next block hanging out of the windows of low-riders, yelling propositions at girls even younger than you, you've seen those old men with their brown bags sitting on the curb in front of the Seven-Eleven store, you've seen those drop-out boys inside at the video machines whispering about the size of your boobs when you're waiting to pay for your bubble gum. I squint my eyes and wave my arms as mother have done for hundreds of years, conjuring up these images until Daughter finally says *all right all right,* even though Fran comes in after midnight and she's all right, she hasn't been beaten up, so what's there to worry about?

Sometimes Daughter does help Fran babysit, she plays with the babies and helps with their baths. Sometimes when I get home from working at the bookstore I tell Fran she can go down to the corner and get herself some cigarettes while I look after the babies a little bit. But mostly I don't help, instead of helping I make rules. After all I am the Lord, right? I am the Lord of the House! I get home tired from working at the bookstore all day, and if I have any energy at all I want to spend it talking to my own kids or even doing some of my writing, I don't want to spend it changing diapers and watching little babies beat each other up and cleaning up dog shit the German shepherd and the little black puppy have laid down. So I say to Pauline, Now there shouldn't be any babies up after ten o'clock because me and my kids have got to get to sleep, see. I say, Now, Pauline, having these dogs upstairs has got to stop because the puppy pisses on Second Son's mattress every chance he gets, so you need to make a fence or get a rope or something so that you can keep them out in the backyard. And I say Now, Pauline, no more babies in my room, okay? Because they get into my papers and tear them up. And Pauline says okay. And I tell the same rules to Fran, and Fran says okay. But you all know the rule about rules, so I don't help but my rules don't help either, and so stew stew stew bubble and brew, dogs shitting on the beds, babies pissing on the kitchen table, stereos, chairs, dishes, everything breaking and nobody knows what to do.

Simon downstairs stops Daughter in the hall. He tells her to tell me that he is going to call the landlord if I don't throw that family out. A couple of days later he stops Fran, he says he is going to call the police if her mother doesn't leave. After that he stops Morgani, he says he is going crazy from all the noise upstairs, that he is going to hold me personally responsible if he flunks school. Finally one evening I am getting home from the bookstore just as he is driving up with Mathias's scowl peeking over the right side of the dashboard. When I see we are going to meet on the porch, just when his eyes begin to narrow but before he can get his words out, I say, hi Simon, how's it going? That's a nice shirt you have on, you sure look great in red, you want to send your kid up to play a little bit tonight?

And he says Oh! All right! while his eyes open up again and his heart leaps involuntarily like any mother's heart will at the thought of free babysitting. Oh, you can't believe what has happened to me, Pat, he says while I lean against my door and give him a little allowance of attention, you know I put an ad in the student newspaper for massage by the hour? Well, this woman with this incredible voice called! And she asked me if I did massage, like my ad said, and I said yes, and she asked if I would mind coming to her house, and I said not at all, and then she said well, can you pick me up where I work? And I said maybe, it depended where it was that she was working, how much gas it would take, and she said, Well, I work at the Playboy Club! Can you imagine that, Pat? He shakes his head like he's having a hard time imagining it himself, me massaging a Bunny!

Well, good luck Simon, I say, you send Mathias up in his pajamas and he can spend the night.

Thanks, Pat, he says, I didn't know exactly what I was going to do with Mathias. I wave, and he's fumbling with his door, he can hardly wait to slap on the aftershave and depart, obviously he's not thinking about the noise upstairs. If he hears any thumps or cries while he's taking his bath and fluffing his chest hair and flexing his fingers, he might think just when he hears it next time I see that Pat I'll say something, I'll give her a piece of my mind, but not tonight, not right now, not when I'm so tired of being a mother, and then goes back to the story of his Playboy evening already unfolding in his mind.

▲

The next morning is Saturday. Pauline told Fran she's going to be home this weekend, but she's up early with a red bandana around her hair, already down the street in Barbie-doll Levi's to bring us donuts from Winchell's and a morning newspaper. I hear a knock on the door and think it might be Mathias come to get the houseslippers and teddy bear he had left on the blanket where he had slept. I had heard him early in the morning before anyone else was up, tiptoeing down the stairs, pounding on his daddy-Simon's door and yelling Let me in! Let me in! mad and worried sounding like he always sounds, until I heard the door open and knew that Simon did get home after all.

But when I open the door, it isn't Mathias, it is a woman who looks to be still in her teens with a broad country face, and yellow hair, and a belly about seven months along.

I'm looking for Pauline Knight, she says when I open the door, looking at me like she thinks I'm the one she's looking for.

I figure this is more of Pauline's trouble, so I say, what do you need her for?

My name is Angela Moore. I came all the way from Tennessee to talk to the woman who put my husband in jail.

Look, I say into her wide country blue eyes, Pauline does not live here. She is only staying temporarily until she finds other quarters. I don't know what your business is with her but you're going to have to deal with her somewhere outside of this house.

Is she in right now?

No.

Well, she says, swinging her heavy body around, I'm just going to sit on this porch step until she comes.

Now I have no idea how long she's going to be.

Oh I'll just sit here and wait, she says. She's sitting on the front step, her girth spread out around her nesting-hen style taking up all the space between the two porch columns. Unbudgeable. She smiles up at me, heavy with child, as they say. I try but I can't think of anything to say to her. Not really. So I don't say anything. I go on up the stairs. Fran and Daughter and the babies are sitting in the middle of the bed watching television. I make myself a cup of instant coffee and walk out on the balcony in my houserobe. Blue jays have built a nest within two feet of the rail. One of them is sitting on it. The other is squawking and dive-bombing the dog from next door. The dog trots through the yard with her tail down. I feel sorry for her because she really isn't doing anything, she can't climb a tree, but then I can understand the watchful mother bird in the nest, worried about the hatching eggs and the father bird full of paranoia. But the father bird relishes his dive-bombing role too much, I think, when he keeps dive-bombing the dog all the way to the end of the block, finally soaring up again through the branches squawking at the mother bird full of his own glory. I hear some voices from the steps below. It's Pauline with the donuts talking to Angela Moore, but I can't hear what they're saying. I sip on my coffee for a while and then go into the house to make some orange juice. Pretty soon Pauline comes in. She's making her agitated-Pauline sounds like hunh! and whew! and well! as though she has been overwhelmed by too much information to spit out in logical sentence forms.

Now who was that? I ask her.

Well! she says. Angela Moore! she says. And to think that guy had a wife! Pauline paces around the little kitchen letting her jaw drop open like there are no words to express her surprise. I can see that here comes another Pauline story, and sure enough, she starts telling me another incredible one while I fish a lemon-filled out of the donut bag.

One day she was over on Gaston Avenue, it was raining and she had just missed her bus. Along comes this guy in a truck, she says, and he asks if I want a ride and I say sure, and so I hop in. He asks where I'm going and I give him the directions. But pretty soon I can see he's not going where I told him to go. So he pulls into an alley and falls on top of me and he's pulling at my clothes! And I'm screaming! So I guess, I don't know, I think he's just nuts, but he must get scared or something, and I'm grabbing at the door handle trying to get out, so he revs the engine up again and takes off. But all the time he's trying to drive and punch me and tear at my clothes all at once, and I'm screaming and he's yelling You cunt! You cunt! And then we're on the freeway and we're going about forty miles an hour and I finally get the door open and jump out—

On the *freeway*?

She nods solemnly. In the center lane, she says, of North-Central Expressway, cars coming from everywhere. First I just hang onto the door as much as I can and then I

156

drop off. The car in back of us sees me hanging on the door first and then when I come down onto the pavement the driver stops and picks me up and takes me to the hospital. And I don't have any broken bones, only pavement burns.

So this Angela Moore is the truck driver's wife?

Pauline nods again. She's mad because I pressed charges. I saw the truck's license plate numbers and the police put him in jail. I mean I'm not a vindictive person, Pat, but I think that man needs to be in prison. I mean he is crazy, he could do that to anybody!

Well, of course!

But that's not what Angela Moore is saying. She wants me to drop the charges against him. She says he's not that kind of guy, he was just too lonely being away from her so long. She says I'm ruining her life.

That's ridiculous!

Oh, I don't know, Pauline says.

She's sitting down at the table, pressing one hand over her eyes. Angela says she'll give me some money.

How much?

Two hundred dollars.

Tell her to go away, I say. I get some eggs out of the refrigerator and scramble them. Willy the baby comes in when he hears the grease popping, with half a donut still in one hand. He tugs on my pants. Pauline is quiet, staring out of the kitchen window. The eggs sizzle and Simon-Polli's voice rumbles through the pipes shouting at Mathias to take his pants off so that he can be given a bath.

I hate you! Mathias shouts.

I hate you too! Simon shouts back.

Then there is the sound of crying and Simon-Polli shouting Shut up! Shut up! while I shovel eggs into a bowl for Willy. Pauline leaves the table to go into the back hall off the kitchen where her mattress is on the floor, shutting the door between the rooms. Willy and I eat the rest of our breakfast to the clicking of Pauline's I Ching coins thrown six times on the other side of the door.

So it is getting to be close to Eastertime. Pauline is like

157

Mother Nature herself flitting in and out of the house while her household grows effortlessly around her, the house vibrating with an enthusiasm for its own fecundity, which I do not share. Babies come up and down the stairs from all over the neighborhood to play with the two babies at our house. Pauline's German shepherd turns out to be pregnant, due to deliver in a matter of weeks. And a blond girl shows up in Morgani's bed, curtailing somewhat the evening practice hours of his guitar, another daughter of Pauline's, a big-boobed teenage girl who's been living with some aunt who wants to kick her out. The phone is always ringing for Pauline: employment agencies, collection agencies, welfare, food stamps, the prosecuting attorney's office for depositions, the Texas Parole Board for statements, and Angela Moore quoting Bible passages about mercy and love. Pauline says one day, Hey Pat, what do you think about the bunch of us rooming together, after I get a job, then I could start giving you some money for rent, that would help you out. But no no, Pauline, no deal and no dice, no wise and no way baby, I mean even in the Bible story Jesus only had to furnish one or two meals at the most out of his baskets of loaves and fishes, the multitude didn't just decide to move in and stay.

Leo calls long distance to make plans for coming up from Galveston for the holiday. He says Is that woman still up there?

I say, Yes but she's going to be gone pretty soon.

By Easter? he says.

I say maybe, but of course I know it probably won't be as soon as that. After I hang up, I start worrying about Leo coming, and I worry he won't like this situation very much at all, since telling him over the telephone that I have been having some house guests doesn't really convey the flavor of the scene. But I figure that I will fix the latch on the bedroom door that one of the babies tore off, and cook a large turkey, maybe that will be something at least.

On Ash Wednesday while I'm on my balcony watching the kids walk home from school, all the Chicanos with grey ritual smears on their foreheads, I suddenly notice a man in the yard looking up at me. Is Pauline Knight up there? he asks.

158

No, she's out.

Well when she comes back, he says, tell her Ray wants to see her.

And I think oh-oh, oh-oh, is that who I think it is? Sure enough, when Pauline comes in, and I say that someone named Ray came by, she says, that's him! That's my ex!

I thought you said he was in California.

Oh no, she says, he came back and he's got an apartment about half a block from here.

I say, well, how did he know you were here?

But she is vague, she's not sure, or maybe one of the kids told him. Oh, and she is worried, she is agitated, she paces around the apartment telling me about the rifle again. Oh he is bound to kill me, she says, you don't know what he's like, he is bound to do me in.

Now Pauline, I say, don't project, maybe he's in a different mood now, we won't let him in the house, we'll get a peace bond, we'll call the cops.

Oh that's nothing, she says, nothing will stop him! Just you wait and see!

That night when everyone's finally asleep and Daughter is tucked in bed beside me, I can't get to sleep myself. I stare at the moonlight coming in through the balcony door. I listen to the wind in the branches outside the window, I look without looking at the darkness hanging between me and the ceiling. Finally I get out of bed. I stand in the middle of the bedroom in my underwear. I breathe in and breathe out. I make my arms go around in a circle. I make my spine relax. I imagine my arms are going in a circle around the house, making an imaginary line, and I imagine all of us inside of it and Ray out. I call out to Ray in the name of every power I can think of—in the name of Mary and Jesus and Father Peyote and electrical power lines and the Rio Grande River—making my arms swing out in a large circle. *Ray Ray Ray Ray don't you cross this power line.* For a few minutes I stand and don't think of anything. I just listen to the sound of all the babies and children and animals in the house breathing in and out.

The next day after Pauline comes home from the

temporary secretary's job she has been working, she asks if Ray can come over for supper.

You've got to be kidding, I say.

Well, he's feeling better, she says. You told me to be calm, so I was calm and we had a drink together, and he's feeling better.

Not a chance, I say.

But he misses Fran, he wants to see her.

No way.

Not even so that Fran can see her father?

Tell him to meet her somewhere, not here. Look, I say, you've spent the past several weeks letting me know what a terror this man is, and I can't change my mind that fast.

Oh, it's just Ray, she says, that's just the way he is.

Well look, Pauline, I finally say, you tell Ray I said there is a line drawn at the first step up the stairs, and I do not want him to cross it. And I tell her this in such a way that she doesn't ask what kind of line, she knows that I *did* draw a line and that whether or not she can see it herself, she can be sure it is there. Tears come to her eyes, but she goes to her room and throws another I Ching and then starts running bathwater for the babies.

I come home from the bookstore on Good Friday an hour early so that I can do a little cleaning before Leo arrives. Ray is on the porch in one of Simon-Polli's lawn chairs with Fran sitting on the wooden arm talking to him. Ray has on a palm-tree shirt and pressed slacks, his hair is slicked back and his face is still pink from a close shave, like he has worked hard to clean up for this visit. When I walk up on the porch he leaps up, standing first on one foot, then another, with his hands deep in both pockets.

Well hey, he says, smiling at me, thanks a lot for what you're doing for Pauline, for my family. But his eyes are everywhere except on me, up and down and over my shoulder, and I think oh-boy he is indeed a squirrelly one, and I don't smile. Well really, I say, it's just between me and Pauline. Then I walk past him as stiff as if I am encased in clacking armor and step over the invisible line at the front step like it is a foot high.

The apartment is rocking like a John Cage concert, every dial turned to ten in every room, punctuated by shouts and crying, buzzing voices. Get out of here! I yell out randomly. Everyone get out of here for a while!

Second Son comes out of his room and thumps the bicycle downstairs, Morgani and Pauline's stray sex-kitten daughter come out of Morgani's bedroom with their faces flushed and their arms around each other. I give the babies a little push down the stairs—go play with Fran on the porch for a little while. Daughter asks if she can eat supper down the street with a friend and skips down every other stair when I say yes. I start sweeping and picking up my dirty clothes. In a little while Fran comes upstairs, but I don't say anything. Then she goes back down the stairs again with two glasses of water. Pretty soon I hear Pauline's laugh outside, and Fran comes upstairs and goes down with another glass. I begin to make up the bed. The apartment is quiet and the voices on the porch seem far away. I run bathwater, lie underneath the soap bubble surface and listen to the sudden quiet which has settled on the house. My flowered robe Leo bought for me in Laredo is hanging on a peg on the back of the door, and when I get out of the tub and towel off, I put it on. When I open the bathroom door, there is only a bit of light in the hallway, the last of the sunset coming through the doorpanes downstairs. Even the voices from the porch are gone and I feel quiet—a few minutes when I am completely alone. But just as I start from the bathroom to my room, I hear the downstairs door click open and I pause on the landing. I peer down the dark stairwell, ready for anything, and flick on the hall light. A beard and broad-brimmed hat peek around the downstairs door—Leo!

Hello baby! he says.

▲

Now I tell you the truth, when Leo comes home from Galveston after being gone so long, I just want to fuck him.

That's all I want to do, I want to screw with him, I want to love him, lie on top of him, lie underneath him or lie right beside him, and I want to lick him, I want to kiss him everywhere, I want to suck on him, and fuck on him, and want him sucking and fucking on me, it's a truth whether it's evil or good, it's all I want to do. And if I had my way I would fuck Leo outside under every bush and in every creek and vacant lot and flower bed along Swiss Avenue, and I would howl like a banshee when I danced my butt up and down his cock. But I am civilized and Leo is civilized, and so we simply go into this quiet bedroom alone together for the first time in a month and put the latch on the door and take our clothes off and get into bed and fit ourselves into one connected self as quickly as possible. We start wrestling around in the bed and kissing, me moaning in Leo's ear and Loe saying unintelligible things when someone tries to open the latched door.

I've gone to bed, I yell out. Leo's here and he's going to sleep, too.

It's Daughter. She knows what I mean. Oh, she says. Okay.

You can get yourself ready for bed, can't you?

She says yes, and goes away from the door. Leo starts tentatively pushing up and down again and I push back but it's not quite so much fun. Every time Leo pushes up and down the noise level outside the door grows a little more. Lights come on in the hallway. Music comes on.

Finally Leo stops. What's that? he says.

What's what? I ask, listening with him to the footsteps up the hallway, one of the babies crying, Pauline talking to Fran, Fran shouting at Pauline, Second Son switching his stereo back on, Simon-Polli's television drifting up from the floorboards, and of course outside the bedroom window above our heads the cooing of pigeons nesting on the roof of the house next door.

What's all that noise? Leo asks. We listen together, lying in each other's arms, to the house turning up the amps to higher and higher levels.

Oh, I say, that's just the kids coming home.

162

Leo's visit goes downhill from there. The babies are crying before the sun comes up in the morning. The telephone rings constantly. Second Son and Morgani won't talk very much to Leo, Daughter talks too much, Simon-Polli calls up and talks to Leo over half an hour telling him all the worst news of what is going on upstairs in that apartment that still has Leo's name on the door. The babies are in their worst and most crying moods. Egg dye, green cellophane grass, bunnie chocolate bits, egg crumbs and Handel's Messiah blasting out Frank Zappa on the stereo. Easter morning and Pauline is awake before the sun rises making dressing with the turkey already in the oven.

When I come into the kitchen she says, See? There's going to be enough for all of us okay!

Who's all of us?

And she says, Well can't Ray come up? Just for today?

And I say no.

Even though I'm cooking the turkey?

She starts crying. Leo comes in. Pauline runs out.

There's a friend of Pauline's at the door, Leo says. I told him he could wait for her inside.

I walk past Leo to see if it is who I think it is. When I sure enough see him in the hall—over the invisible line!—I stop and glare. Ray, you'd better go on out.

I just wanted to use the phone.

I don't even say no, I just shake my head. He does go out. But I am suddenly confused. There is a line for Ray but Leo is in the house. And why am I refusing to have Easter dinner with Pauline and her ex-old man? And if I have three children and an ex-old man, too, and then if I have Leo and some fun with Leo, then why can't Pauline have some fun on Easter too? And then it is Easter after all. The truce of spring! And why all these rules? In the middle of the fog I remember it's because of the rent—because Pauline doesn't pay it, although she has wanted to, but I don't want her to, I just don't. And then the utilities, too, I gather up all the money and pay the utilities, too, I write all the checks myself. I name off the utilities one at a time—gas, electric, water and telephone—like saying a line of beads on a rosary, until the confusion clears and I can move again out of the empty hall.

Leo doesn't want to eat Easter dinner in the apartment, so we make a big sack of food, and Second Son, Morgani, Daughter, Leo and I carry all the stuff downstairs to load in the truck. We have a good meal at the park in the grass listening to an outdoor band, and then we head back home. Outside on the porch Ray is sitting on the lawn chair with a big piece of turkey Pauline brought down for him, and Angela Moore is sitting on the steps talking to Pauline, looking ripe as a two-month nesting egg, and the babies are scooting and squealing around Ray's legs. We walk through them and say something about Easter and the weather. I think well, it is a pleasant day, they are making happy sounds, Leo has had a good time after all, he hasn't said anything one way or another. But when we get upstairs Leo shuts the door to the bedroom and explodes.

Didn't you tell me once, he says, that the trouble with your first marriage was that you were always inviting people to live with you? Didn't you say one of the reasons that marriage fell through was because of that?

Well, I tell him, it wasn't *the* reason why that marriage fell through—

You'd better get that woman out of here, Leo says, she'd better be out of here by the end of the month or I'm not going to pay my part of the rent anymore.

Oh, she's going to be out the first of the month.

I mean it, Pat, he says, the idea! You moving all these people into the house while I'm away.

At least it keeps me from getting lonely, I say.

But Leo doesn't think that's a bit funny. He packs up. He kisses me good-bye but he is angry. Happy risen Christ getting the hell out of here hitting the road again to single-man heaven.

So Leo is gone. He hasn't even stayed long enough to leave his smell on my sheets. Squashed eggs in the hall. Even my used-to-belong-to-Grandmaw rocker has come loose at one of its legs so that when I sit out on my balcony watching

Leo back out of the driveway, I sit half-sliding out of the seat. And I think Leo shouldn't have tried to threaten me, it doesn't matter if I have his money for the rent or not. But I don't blame him, I want this Pauline story to end myself, I don't want to be around when the husband gets out of prison and finds the ex-husband on the front porch, or when Fran finally finds what she's looking for when it's stuck up inside her, I don't want to hear what happened this time on Pauline's way to work, I don't want to walk through the house anymore through broken toys and stereo sets and spilled milk and dog piss and I don't want to deliver any half-German shepherd puppies! And why should Leo finally take his name off the mailbox because of this whim of mine to come down from the balcony one evening dressed up in god-clothes forgetting to bring a change of costume? And why *can't* I be the Salvation Army? Why doesn't anyone ever listen to MY rules? Why do the goddamn babies keep coming into my room and painting themselves with my liquid paper? I sit and brood watching the nesting pigeons under the eaves of the other roof. I mean, how can they sit there so long when the sky is blue, how can they know when to give up if the eggs aren't hatching?

▲

One day just like in the old movies the news finally comes, the dust of the rescue squad appears on the horizon, the sun comes through the clouds, the late chicks hatch out of their eggs late for Easter but still in time for life, and Pauline has gotten herself a house.

Pauline has gotten herself a house! Somehow in the midst of dealing with babies and dogs and checking out want ads and showing up for various jobs, and getting fired and getting hired and going for drinks with friends when the going got too heavy, and trying to find where Fran is going at night and trying to keep Ray out of the house and visiting two prisons in two different towns every week, Pauline has managed to find a house, Pauline has done all of that. With a little bit of help—Angela Moore is going to share the rent.

165

Ray is going to live in the garage until the husband gets paroled. Whatever. Still, Pauline is on her way out.

The night Pauline comes home with the news is the night Simon-Polli comes to deal with me straight out. He's squinching his forehead up and shoveling his mustache up in his nose trying to look his most pitiful. I'm going crazy, he says, I stopped at a stoplight this morning and put my head on my arms, Pat, and I cried—I just cried!

Well, Simon,—I pat him on the back—you don't have to worry anymore. Pauline has gotten herself a house. Pretty soon she's going to be moving out.

He looks a little stunned, a little confused when I say that. But then he slumps down again. Oh it's not just Pauline, he says, it's my son, he's so hateful, I tell him to do things and all he says is no. And my friends won't have anything to do with me anymore because they're all single and I have this son.

Well still, Simon, I say trying to cheer him up, not everybody gets to massage Playboy bunnies—

His face crumbles with pain. Oh Pat, he says, it was just a joke! There wasn't any Playboy bunny! I went to pick her up and gave her name at the desk and there was nobody like that working there.

You want to smoke a joint? I ask him.

You got one?

Sure, I say. I take him out on the balcony where a light breeze has begun to come in through the branches and we light up.

It'll get better, I tell him.

How's that?

It just will, I say. Behind us I can hear Simon's son laughing with Willy-the-baby over something, but with the door closed I can't hear what they're talking about. We pass the joint back and forth for a while, and then we just sit on our balcony perch watching out through the leaves at the street traffic passing, listening to the cooing and chortling coming from the eaves of the rooftop next door, Simon and me quiet, for tonight letting the pigeons have the last word.